my
heart
is a
mountain

my
heart
is a
mountain

tales of magic and the land

Catherine Holm

HOLY COW! PRESS :: DULUTH MINNESOTA :: 2011

10 9 8 7 6 5 4 3 2 1

We gratefully acknowledge the following publications in which these stories first appeared:
"Transcendence," *Electric Velocipede,* Issue 2, Spring 2002; "Detours," *Electric Velocipede,*
Issue 15/16, Winter 2008; "The Last Great Chance," *Electric Velocipede,* Issue 3, Fall 2002;
and "Crossroads," originally published at www.strangehorizons.com, July 14, 2003 and
reprinted in the Polish magazine *Tawacin,* 2004. "Farmwoman" was a finalist in
Minnesota Magazine's 2010 fiction contest.

Catherine Holm is a fiscal year 2010 recipient of an Artist Support Grant from the
Arrowhead Regional Arts Council (www.arcouncil.org) which is funded by the Minnesota
Arts and Cultural Heritage Fund as appropriated by the Minnesota State Legislature with
money from the vote of the people of Minnesota on November 4, 2008; an appropriation
from the Minnesota State Legislature; and the McKnight Foundation.

Library of Congress Cataloging-in-Publication Data

Holm, Catherine Dybiec.
My heart is a mountain : tales of magic and the land / by Catherine Holm.
p. cm.
ISBN 978-0-9823545-5-1 (alk. paper)
1. United States--Social life and customs--Fiction. I. Title.
PS3608.O494323M94 2010
813'.6—dc22   2010023165

Holy Cow! Press books are distributed to the trade by
Consortium Book Sales & Distribution, c/o Perseus Distribution
1094 Flex Drive, Jackson, Tennessee 38301

For personal inquiries, write to
Holy Cow! Press
Post Office Box 3170
Mount Royal Station
Duluth, Minnesota 55803
Please visit our website: www.holycowpress.org

To Chris, my partner and husband,
who helped make this possible.
Thank you—I love you!

contents

9   Disappearing Men

19   Saving Grace

27   My Heart is a Mountain

37   The Last Great Chance

51   Crossroads

67   Everywhere

73   Heart Armor

85   Transcendence

93   The Day Jaded Came to Town

103   Detours

113   Dad's Rural Genes (a memoir)

117   Farmwoman

123   About the Author

disappearing men

"You're doing it again," Clara said, glaring at her husband, hands on her hips, fingers thin and mottled from sixty-seven years of life on Earth and infinite days of doing dishes.

"What?" Edward looked up from his armchair that faced the TV.

"Closing off. Leaving me." How could the man be so dense? Where did he go when he disappeared from the living room they'd shared for fifty years of marriage?

Edward materialized completely, coming back into focus so that Clara could make out the sheen of his bald scalp. The top of his head looked oily and uncared for. She couldn't remember the last time she'd touched him there.

The ring finger on her right hand twitched, and she flicked it against her yellow apron; "Mom Loves to Cook!" the apron proclaimed. Cooking was a necessary chore. Edward had schemed to give her the apron, she'd decided, to keep her in the kitchen.

"Where do you go when you do that?" The tone in her voice was more demanding than she'd intended, but it was too late to take it back now. She saw the familiar fuzziness overtake him. This time, it started on his shoulder, traveling down the outline of his arm. His arm disappeared, then his neck, one half of his head, and finally, his entire head.

"Edward!"

Too late. He was off again wherever he went when he didn't want to face her; when he didn't want to look at life.

. . .

Clara couldn't keep the irritation out of her voice. "Every time I try to bring up something he doesn't want to hear, he disappears."

Norma nodded, sympathy plain across her broad, Nordic face. They drank coffee, sitting at Clara's butcher-block table.

"Money, the kids, grandkids on drugs, house repairs—"

"Men can't deal with the world, honey." Norma dumped sugar into her coffee cup and clanked the spoon against the porcelain. "Burt's been doing it too."

Clara raised her eyebrows.

Norma sighed. "As if they don't have it good enough."

"Exactly." Clara slammed her fist on the table, and Norma stiffened with a surprised look. "They've always had their woods, their deer hunting, their alone time, their coffee in the morning with the guys. How much more alone can they get?" She swept her arm past the window, indicating the view outside. Acres of marsh and woods stretched to the horizon. "What are they running from?"

"Try to figure out the mind of a man." Norma shrugged and pushed away a plate of crumbcake.

. . .

When Edward disappeared, he didn't stop to think about what happened. He enjoyed the sensation. He had a faint memory of his wife's grating voice trying to pull him back as he faded out.

Why should he care how it transpired? The end result mattered most, as long as he got away.

He always materialized into a large cabin. The rustic pine paneling suggested that men had created this place. It occurred to him that the cabin might be a composite dream, a vision that the group of men gathering here made their own reality.

Edward looked out the window of the cabin at the pine and spruce forest: familiar, yet different. Unearthliness tinged everything and gave it a blur around the edges. He wondered if his buddies noticed.

"Hey, Edward."

He turned. An old table sat in the middle of the cabin with six guys around it. Paint-spattered chairs provided seating, the kind of chairs that might hang from the rafters in a musty garage. *Six guys? That's more than usual.* Edward wore his coveralls, the ones Clara hated and had threatened to throw away.

"Hi, all. What's on the menu?" He shuffled over and sat down.

"Same as always, whatever you want."

A few of the men laughed as a plate of hash and eggs materialized in front of Edward. Clara hounded him about his cholesterol intake.

"Yummm." He dug in. "What's the plan for the day?"

"Same as usual—a little ice fishing, hunt some deer, sit around, drink coffee."

"Sounds good." Edward took a swallow from a coffee cup that had appeared in front of him. Just right, not too strong, not too weak, and black.

Edward went back to the real world for a number of reasons: a chainsaw needed fixing, snow needed to be shoveled, the dog needed care, but more and more, he spent time at the cabin where there were no demands, no problems. He didn't understand women. Why did they have to make things complicated with their questions? Why couldn't they just ride the waves of life and let it be?

. . .

Clara wondered if her life resembled the dishrag in her hand—limp and without purpose. She thought of her days as stepping stones, random water-breaks in a rushing stream. The dark water around the stones splashed with risk, scariness, the unknown. The water hinted at beauty, but at what cost? The stones were safer, to be sure, but predictable. She could rail at Edward all she wanted for avoiding life's risks, but she knew she wasn't perfect in that respect either, and she hadn't mastered the art of disappearing. Clara snapped the dishrag against the counter, taking perverse pleasure in watching a sprig of water arc into the air. She wondered if this constituted a step off the stones. The phone rang.

Edward's voice came through on the other end. It sounded fuzzy and distant. The connection hissed and popped.

"Don't forget to give Molly her heartworm pill."

"I don't know where her pills are. Where are you?"

"Pills are in the tool shed, top shelf. Vet says she needs one in November. Still a chance she could get bit by a mosquito."

Clara had swatted one a few days ago, watching it burst in a pin-sized spray of blood on her upper arm. She could swear they were getting more aggressive. "Where are you?" she repeated.

Edward's voice sounded dreamy through the distortion. "It's nice here. Nothing to do but fish and hunt and talk with the guys. Think...I'll...stay." The spaces between his words stretched as if he talked through a haze, as if each vowel, noun, and verb pushed through thick fog.

Anger surged up in Clara. A geyser burst up in her chest, and she remembered a picture of Yellowstone's Old Faithful in a weathered edition of *National Geographic*.

How could he leave when she was faced with the realities of everyday life? There he sat—wherever he was—because he couldn't deal with what life doled out to him here. All the more ridiculous because his life was pretty damned good.

"How can you sit and talk about escaping?" The words volleyed out of her mouth, cannonballs on fire.

"What?"

"You can't stand reality." Her voice rose half an octave, the creaky overtones of old age simmering around the words. "Who raised eight kids? Who ran this house? Gardened and canned? Nursed sick animals and children and you? Made it pleasant for you when you came home, even if my day was crummy? That's reality."

"Clara—"

She could hear his voice starting to fade away and knew that he was leaving. Clara muffled a hysterical laugh, wondering if he was running from his own fantasy because of her demands.

"I'm coming to find you!"

She slammed down the phone, barely noticing how it bounced in its cradle from the shock of her force.

.   .   .

She got it wrong first. Locating Edward's reality required refinement. The mind was more active and ambitious than Clara imagined. She'd made herself sit down in Edward's armchair and picture a place free of worries. When she opened her eyes, she sat in their house.

She stood up, wondering if the floor would hold her, and she didn't fall through. Her eyes traveled over the spotless kitchen that adjoined the living room. No dishes in the sink. On an impulse, she swung open the closet door where a purple apron hung. She pulled the material to its full width:

"When I am old, I shall not do dishes."

Her eyes sparkled like a child's. Clara's lips spasmed, holding back delight. She slammed the door and skittered through the rest of the house. Someone very interesting lived there. She could tell by the collection of CDs stacked under the stereo.

A piano sat in the living room. Her heart trembling, she

tottered toward it on unsteady feet. Difficult music perched in stacks on the instrument—music she could play years ago before she stopped practicing and got rid of the piano. When her eyes locked on the handwritten piece that sat on the stand, she felt her breath catch and stop. *My signature.* "I wrote this," she whispered.

Clara almost couldn't read the penciled notes through the water that welled in her eyes. Later, she had no memory of pulling out the bench, sitting on it with knees like liquid. Her hands traveled over the keys as if she knew the music, though she couldn't figure out how she could play it. The rendition was rough and unpracticed, but she caught the essence of the composition. Her composition grew from the keys as it must have morphed from her mind.

It would be nice to stay here. When she had dealt with Edward, maybe she would come here again. She went to sit in the armchair and willed herself into Edward's world instead of her own.

. . .

Edward rubbed the sand from his eyes and rolled off the narrow bunk bed. Somehow, the cabin seemed more noisy than usual, particularly the dining area, from which he heard a large amount of clattering. And, he could have sworn there were more bunk beds in this room. He pulled on coveralls from a heap on the floor. There'd be time to shave later, or maybe he'd just let it grow.

"What's for breakfast?"

"Tofu scramble. Christ, I can get better food at home."

Tofu scramble? Edward felt his stomach churn. Tofu reminded him of bar soap. He approached the dining table. There were more men indeed, some he didn't recognize. Among the strangers was the one responsible for ordering the soap-bar scramble, no doubt.

"Can't a guy get some decent food around here?" A plate of bacon, eggs, and hash browns materialized on the table just as the picture flashed through his mind. "That's more like it," he muttered. He dug in, but with less ease than usual. The constant talk distracted him.

"Hey, Bob," he said, nudging his neighbor, "hard to eat with all this noise, huh?"

Bob nodded. Edward had known him since grade school, a one-room building in the country. Edward ate and listened to the conversation around him.

"Good time to sell…"

"Yeah, I'll take a loss…"

"Long-term growth…"

"Where'd they come from?" he said to Bob, not bothering to lower his voice.

His neighbor shrugged. "More and more men want to come here. Gettin' too crowded for my taste."

Edward agreed. He looked around. The walls shone as if they'd been dusted. The chairs no longer creaked with the rickety softness of age and worn wood. Pretty soon, the place would have a cappuccino bar. He was afraid to look out the window. What would replace his spruce and tamarack forests? Paved suburbs? The stench of a belching city?

He stared at his plate. The hash browns were gone, as was the bacon he hadn't eaten. A heap of yellow stuff—like those fake eggs Clara made—occupied the center of the plate. Next to them sat a piece of wheat toast, unbuttered.

He swung around and heard Clara's snapping voice.

"Edward, I told you not to eat that junk. It's bad for your heart."

"What are you doing here?" Edward could see confusion, then panic, in the faces of the men around the table. The furniture shifted and changed before their eyes, becoming newer and cleaner. Plates of fake eggs and dry toast appeared on the table in front of the men. The tofu scramble remained unchanged. Edward noticed it belonged to one of the stock-spouting yuppies.

"Christ," Bob muttered, "this stinks." And then he vanished, most likely home to his wife. Home was better than dealing with this shifting dream that couldn't decide what it wanted to be. Many of the men disappeared before Edward could say a word. The stock market bunch remained, all four of them.

Clara glared at them. "My husband and I have business."

They faded out. *So much for the gutless wonders.*

She didn't waste time. "What is this place?"

"What was it, you mean." He exhaled, reluctant to let out a breath that felt like his dream slipping away. Where had the old guy-camaraderie gone? Changed instantly by too many men, and his wife.

"Why do you have to come here? What's so wrong with your life?" Clara demanded.

Speech escaped Edward. How could he explain it? A safe haven where men could go was sacred—like church for some, like a tree house of his youth with a "NO GIRLS" sign over the entrance.

"This was a good place," he muttered. "No pressures. Time with the guys."

She gestured with her arms, and Edward had a quick vision of the girl he'd fallen in love with, always trim, always sharp.

"You can have time with the guys where we live. What do you have to come here for?" Her voice had a clipped tone.

"It's different."

"How?"

He stared at her. He didn't know. True, he could escape with the guys in any number of ways. They had started to come here, and it'd turned into a habit. He rolled the last word around in his thoughts. *Habit... only a ... habit ...*

The cabin faded from view, disappearing around them. No walls, no table, no dry eggs, no outside. Only blackness.

· · ·

Clara looked good in her purple apron. Edward thought he'd never seen a better looking sixty-seven-year-old woman. How'd she manage to keep herself in such good shape? Even shapeless fleece sweatpants flattered her. Her butt and legs were trim. His heart started to race, his cheeks heated red. *Careful, you're an old man*, he told himself.

"What're you grinning about?" Clara stood over him, hands out to take his plate.

His mouth watered with the recent memory of eggs, hash, bacon, and thickly buttered toast, right here in his living room. "Nothing, hon."

She rumpled her fingers against the top of his head the way he liked, as if hair still grew there.

"What're you up to today?" she asked. He heard the clatter of plates as she loaded them into the dishwasher.

"Off with the guys. Getting together at Brandy's shack."

"Sounds nice."

The woman was amazing, a constant bundle of energy. The dishwasher gurgled, beginning its cycle. Clara trotted toward the other room, and Edward heard the clack of wood as she raised the cover over the piano keys and began to play music he'd never heard before.

saving grace

"What's your name, hon?" you said.

Smoke hung in the air behind your head. Dark walls made the small bar look cozy, except for the howl of the wind. Had to be forty degrees in this leaky building or worse. Your breath rose in front of your face. Two guys shot pool behind me, and the balls smacked together like ice. A Bud Light sign blinked on one wall; a neon woman with a tiny waist and huge hips wore a bikini and carried a pitcher of beer.

"I don't tell everyone my name," I said to you.

Your smile was something between a hungry sled dog and a grizzly. I shoulda known better than to sit at the bar, but in Alaska, everyone's fair game. I didn't know that then; a greenie.

You were too young and good lookin' to be flirting with me. I'm a plain woman with eyes close together, mousy hair that looks bad whatever I do to it, and big spaces between my teeth. My saving grace is I'm tall and lean; can't put weight on if I try.

I'd crossed from Canada to Alaska several days earlier in my ancient car. I nursed a beer. You ordered a cup of coffee. The bartender, an old native with a broad face, poured you some brew that looked like motor oil.

"That's okay, hon," you said. "Don't need to know your name."

Something tender rose in your voice. I looked at the counter before you could see my face. Formica made bubbles, wetted and rotted by many beers.

A pool ball shattered ice. "Fuck, YEAH!" cried one of the players.

I looked up.

We exhaled, and our breath made white mist in front of our faces. I had wool gloves on—the kind with the top of the fingers cut off. I rubbed my hands together through the wool. I wondered how people could stand to be constantly cold.

"So you's gonna live in the bush?" you said.

A wolf glinted at me from those eyes.

I didn't wonder how you knew. The whole town likely knew my story. Alaska was the strangest place, a small-town and huge all at once.

I set my mouth, stared you straight in the face. "Yep."

"Not too smart, a greenhorn goin' into the bush."

I didn't break my stare.

"You got the clothes? The supplies? You can die out there, easy. This ain't no place to play around."

"I know that."

The pool guys grew quiet, tryin' to listen to us talking.

"Don't suppose you got a gun. Need one out here. If a grizz' gets you, won't be enough left to scrape up and bury."

"I got guns. I use 'em," I said firmly.

But you was looking at the strands of gray hair poking out from my orange wool cap.

"You ain't young." You blinked and took a deep breath. The wolfish eyes grew warm. I wished I was a grizzly; I'd eat you up.

"How old?" you asked softly.

I shook my head. "Ain't telling you my name, and I'll be

damned if I tell you my age."

Wind blasted the outside of the bar, and the metal walls made noises I never heard before.

. . .

I didn't tell you I lived in the bush in the lower forty-eight for many years. To an Alaskan, there ain't no bush in the lower states. I always been single; my lover was the trees and the outside, the big pines and Doug firs and the quiet where I carved out my homestead. I took seasonal work and lived on little: berry picking, tree planting. When it started to get crowded, I had to get out. Alaska, the only wild place left.

I didn't tell you any of that, but beer has a way of making the words slide out one's mouth. You were drinking beer, too, after the cup of sludge you started with. I let my age slip.

"You don't look sixty-five," you muttered. "More like forty or forty-five." You took off your hat, shook out longish hair, brown with red glints. I knew you wasn't lying. I got one of those faces, ugly but ageless. Your jaw got tight; you jutted out your lips. "You gonna need help."

I glared at you. A new song started up on a creaky jukebox. "Sixty-five ain't old," I said. "Age is in your mind."

. . .

I ran into you least once a day. Didn't mind the company. I had no love to give you, or anyone, but I'd cross that bridge if it came to it.

You told me about some land, a one-sixty deep in the bush, surrounded by mountains, a creek running through it. "Take us a day to snowshoe in." Someone would drive us to the trailhead so we could get an early start. We'd camp overnight.

And something started buzzing in my chest, and a warm burn meandered down my throat like bourbon. Gentle snow fell; we stood in front of the general store. I felt a flake settle on my eye lashes.

I smiled, forgetting my teeth. Your eyes held me like a low tundra sun. Your hair glinted with melting snowflakes.

.   .   .

We started out in the dark before sunrise. You knew the trail. You was lookin' at a parcel off this trail yourself, a place where you could start your own homestead.

"Don't buy no closer n' eight miles," I warned you. But you just looked at me as if I'd told you the weather.

"Understand you need your room," you said. "You're in the right place."

We didn't waste time. We'd start losing daylight early afternoon. We carried camping gear in backpacks and pistols on belts; you brought your rifle. Might be that there was an old abandoned cabin on the land; if we found it, we'd sleep in it.

"Damn, woman," you said, "I can hardly keep up with you."

Lots of things I didn't tell you, Red. Might never.

"Sure you never done this before?" you huffed. I was breakin' trail, heavy snow at least two feet deep. The snowshoes sank down at least a foot with each step I took.

"I've lived out. Only way I can survive."

I didn't tell you about the beach town I grew up in, where looks mattered and guys only stared at the pretty girls and all the kids except me hung out in the malls. I didn't tell you I never took no lovers. I could keep you at a distance, but you didn't seem to mind. You were like Alaska, big and contained, all at once.

"Look out ahead," you muttered. "We're here."

I looked out and breathed. I was so still I coulda been one of the trees in this forest, one of the old spruce or tall white pines. I coulda been the snow, untouched and white on the ground, except for our tracks.

"I know this place," I whispered. You looked at me, but my mind jumped back to years before, sitting with a book open on my lap, looking at a centerfold of an Alaska valley: a valley like this, with mountains and a pink-tinged horizon; the flat path of a creek, now frozen and covered with snow; tall conifers; quiet so loud it roared.

We slept in the abandoned cabin that night, not touching. You gave me my space. The land crept into me, a greedy lover.

. . .

"Eight miles," I told you. "Don't come no closer." *My heart's closed, and I don't know how to love.*

You nodded, but I could feel your love coming, building like a hot stream. I called you Red and never learned your real name. You called me Grace since I wouldn't tell you mine. I thought it was funny. Never thought of myself as graceful. Strong and capable, but grace belonged to the blondes on the beach in California; the blondes who never stepped the wrong way in the sand; the blondes the guys couldn't stop watching. The way you looked at me, Red, I'd swear I was the most beautiful girl on the planet.

You helped me build my homestead. We repaired the cabin and started a woodpile and got a garden going. It was as if I'd opened that book that I'd read as a girl and stepped into the pages. You was gone a bit, working on your own homestead eight miles away. But one late afternoon, alone, I stood in my valley, and my heart choked up. The sky was pink and golden around the rims and the hoarfrost glared from the branches of evergreens. I stood for the longest time as the sky grew darker. I jumped and paced to keep warm, and I couldn't take myself inside, even though a fire crackled within the cabin and sent orange shifting against the window. The sky began to dance. Northern Lights poured down, purple and blue and green tendrils of light, coming up to me and backing away.

. . .

I would watch you splitting wood, your shoulders knotting as you brought the maul down, smashing the log down the middle. It'd crack in the cold winter temps, the best time to split wood. I'd feel my own heart tugging as if it wanted to split apart and let you in. We never talked about age. Didn't seem to matter to you, and I didn't let it matter to me. I guessed you in your forties. You were fit, and your eyes had the brightness of a younger man, but harder and older too.

"You didn't need to put up a homestead on account a me," I told you.

"Always wanted to live in the bush." Your voice had the *chuff chuff* sound a bear makes. "Never had a reason before."

"Red."

You put down the maul, kicking aside a split piece of wood. It slid easily over new snow.

"I told you, I don't know how to love. Don't know how to let anyone in. Wasn't born with the lovin' gene, I guess."

You touched one finger to my face. It was as if those Northern Lights came dancing down, even though it was the height of the short day. They twined around my heart. Electricity shot through it. I shut my eyes. Suns burst into yellow/orange flames behind my eyelids.

My breath pushed out, short, uneven. I took a deep inhale, and the cold air coated my heart.

"I'll damage you." My voice was low, the growl of a wolf. "I'll hurt you. Why're you doin' this? I got nothing to give you. I'm empty. Ain't nothing inside me."

You touched me again, one gloved finger on my cheek. "You're wrong," you said. "The land's inside you. I seen it fill you up."

I turned from you, Red, my back to your face. I looked at the pines and spruces. Their needles were my arms; the snow was my breath; and you were the Northern Lights that danced down inside me.

. . .

Fifteen years ago on this day, Red, I touched you for the first time.

For the last time.

I'm in my bed, an orange quilt pulled up around me and damn it, the Northern Lights are dancing outside. The fire's twisting in the woodstove, shooting flames against the glass and cast-iron door.

It was a day like this, frigid January, that we took you in the woods. And a few days before, I heard the news on my radio. We all got radios out here to get messages from town.

You'd been killed by a truck. Five years after we met. Five years of building each others' homesteads and calling each other Red and Grace and letting Alaska become our lover.

The Northern Lights outside are reaching for my heart. I get up, throw another log on the fire, pull on my jacket and boots, step outside.

You'd gone into town for supplies, and you was beginning the long trek back into our bush. You hadn't turned off onto the old logging trail yet, didn't have your snowshoes on. A logging truck came over the hill, loaded with wood. It lost control; the driver dead of a heart attack. He hit you from behind. You never heard him coming, or you heard him coming too late. There's a weather pattern where it's cloudy and there's a fine snowfall and it's hard to hear anything. I wonder if you were thinking of me when you died. I wonder what I was to you—the beauty of ice coming undone as it melts in the spring and the creek comes alive? The frigid and fiery Alaska sunset? The hoarfrost that clings to the branches of the trees, its lover?

We gathered at your homestead, and we said words over you and left you in the deep woods, what you would have wanted.

And I dared, for the first time, to touch your face. When the others had gone, I stroked your cold, leathery skin with my index finger.

Your cheek was white and frozen, and something in my heart came unhinged and I thought the hot stream of it might pour right out of me. I thought I might burst into a million suns, the heat was so intense.

Them in town who know me check on me a few times a year. They bring me supplies, and I go into town too. Gotta be more careful is all, take it slower. Seems I was blessed with endurance, even though I never got any better-looking. I ain't afraid of dying; I ain't afraid of much. It's the gift of age; things matter or don't matter, and fear don't matter much at all. I plan to die the same way we put you in the forest, Red. When I can't go any longer, I'll drag this body into the woods, sit down, and let the cold or the bears take the life from me. Plenty of ways to die in Alaska. And I got the feeling, Red, I am going to die under the Northern Lights. Because that is where I see you.

I see your face clearest when it's forty or fifty below, and the Northern Lights dance over the valley. My heart is the open tundra, wild and dangerous. I open my heart to you now, facing the Alaska sky in my valley, my forest, my cabin. Alaska is nobody's but her own.

my heart is a mountain

I haven't been home for thirty years, but I'm driving up the mountain, going to Ma's as cancer ends her life. There's a bitter ache from my throat to my uterus, like a trapped stream. Sun plays over the ridge of the mountaintop, making wide shadows and looking warm and sharp. A view opens up, and my breath cascades from my face. Wet, rotted leaves bring a flash of memories; walking down these hills, the smell of wood smoke. The trees close around me, the view gone, and I creep up the hill. The mountains are whispering songs I didn't know I could hear.

. . .

Ma's cabin might as well have grown from the soil and the trees around it. It's small; one story, sixteen by sixteen feet. After thirty years, it's shabbier than I remember. Rotted siding meets dirt, and the barn board door is weathered to a dull gray.

There's a chill in the air as I grasp the old metal door handle. It creaks open, and the yeasty smell of cancer pervades the cabin.

A hand pump hangs over the kitchen sink, and oil lamps will be lit when the sun goes down.

A hospice nurse explains medicines and schedules. She leaves, and I'm alone with Ma.

Ma coughs. Her bed has been dragged onto the porch for the last days of her life so she can have the view of Blue Holler. My eyes are drawn to the window. A new road dissects the valley, and trees are felled where Ed Colby's homestead used to be. The path down the holler and into town passed Colby's land. He would give us eggs and homemade wine after Daddy left.

Ma's inhales sound like the rasp of water over rocks, a high mountain stream. She's covered with Grandma's hand-stitched quilt; squares of blue, light blue, white. Ma looks as if she could shrink right into the bed. The yeast smell blends with stale urine.

My fingers are trembling. I put my hands on her shoulders and lean down to hug her. She shrugs me off.

"Where's Sylvia?" she mutters into her pillow.

I turn away, and Blue Holler is a blurry ocean. I press my hands against my stomach. My heart is too big for my chest.

"Ain't much of a view, is it?" she mutters.

I force myself to talk. "What happened to Colby's place?"

She looks at me with eyes too sharp for the dying. "Eminent domain," she spits. "County fell for a condo deal."

Billboards jumped from the side of the road when I got close to my hometown. "Appalachia Dreams! A Five-Million-Dollar View!" Those roads are slicing my heart into pieces, as if my heart is a mountain. How could I not hear it in Jim Feeny's voice when he called me to tell me Ma was dying? There's a language between mountain people, and I can't speak it anymore. The billboards were like every sign I see in the city, every neon display.

"What happened to Colby?" I ask.

Anger keeps Ma alive. It flashes out of her eyes like lightning.

"Family stuck him in a nursing home. Said an old man shouldn't be living alone in a backwoods cabin." Venom's coming from her words like snakes slithering through these woods.

"He hung himself," she hisses. "Two days ago. Take a man's land, and he got nothing."

I can't swallow. "He had a life."

"What do you know? You ain't dying." She's crying, bitter tears wetting a pillow, and I'm thinking about Ed Colby, dead, with no home and no land.

.   .   .

The bulldozers are hammering into the heart of the mountains. I sleep on an old green couch in the living room, and the light wakes me up at five. But at seven a.m., the *bam bam* of dozers and a jackhammer rape the air and the quiet of Blue Holler. Ma winces each time the hammer pounds into the earth, drilling through rock to put in foundation footings. Ed Colby's cabin is buried somewhere. They hauled off the scrap, but there are pieces that will never leave: nails, bits of wood, chicken wire, chicken manure. Colby's roosters' screams echoed across the valley. For a moment, I am Ed Colby, old and bent, sitting on a bed in a nursing home, smelling skin and fouled sheets. A hanger blessedly cuts me from the longing for my homestead and land.

.   .   .

The nurse comes once a day for an eight-hour shift, making the trek up the mountain. She's a local and doesn't turn her nose up at the outhouse or water pump, things I took for granted growing up.

Ma is speaking less.

"They go within," the nurse tells me. "They stop talking, sleep more, eat less."

Ma has seen spirits.

"Where's Sylvia?" she whispers. She blinks at me and turns

away, glowering.

The bulldozer roars in the valley. My apartment, my job, my friends are farther away than Ed Colby, far enough to be on the other side of the Earth. City memories flash through my mind, but they leave quickly—white takeout cartons stained yellow from a spicy sauce, orange Formica kitchen counters. The memories trickle down a mountain, away from me.

"Ma," I say, "Sylvia is dead."

"She's alive," Ma whispers. "I hear her." There's spittle on the quilt near Ma's chin. "Listen."

My ears strain, reaching for the whisper of a three-year-old sister's voice, looking for the glint of blonde hair or a perfect, smooth leg.

"She's there," whispers Ma, "but she won't come to me."

The bulldozer rattles the porch windows.

.   .   .

Sylvia tied me to these mountains. I loved her as I never loved anyone else. When I was twelve and she was two, we walked through the field and woods, our hands warm together. "Plantain," I'd say. "Yellowroot. Ginseng. Creasy greens."

Sylvia laughed and jumped. Light poured from her face. She grabbed the small leaves in her fingers, ripping them from their stems. "Cress!" she shrieked, laughing, and she bit into the peppery leaves. I held her as the mountains held us.

When Sylvia got sick and died, Ma cried from a bottomless pool, as if she had cared for Sylvia the same way she never cared for me.

.   .   .

I'm sitting on a chair next to the bed, half asleep with exhaustion. I don't know when I sleep or wake now, between the bulldozer noise and Ma's care.

"I'm glad to be dyin'," Ma whispers. She's talking to the air, not to me. Her eyes look straight ahead at nothing.

I can't think of anything to say.

"They ripping up these mountains," she says.

There's cars on that road that dissects the holler, more cars than I've ever seen around here. I'm amazed at all the stuff I remember.

· · ·

"Never plant cabbage under a full or waning moon. The trees will talk if you know how to listen. They talk before a storm. Go outside and quiet your mind and hear them. A bit of catnip mint is a tonic for a colicky baby." These were the things Ma said, but the mountain was my teacher. Ma mouthed the words her ma had mouthed to her. The mountains did the teaching.

· · ·

When I can't stand Ma's coughing anymore and the smell of cancer smothers me, I walk out the door, feet pushing through moist and rotting leaf litter. Browns and oranges and yellows make a half-digested muck on the ground. The bulldozer rings through the valley, rising over my ears. There's a vise around my head, pressing in, like two bands of metal where the ends must meet. My feet and knees shake; I keep climbing. Up on a bluff, the roof of Ma's shack pokes through the trees. I imagine the trees and the old foundation ripped up, and the garden patch dug into, and the outhouse and house walls torn down and hauled down the mountain in a truck and taken to the dump. The dump is full of history: a piece of a brass bed from Erma's house; an old enamel sink from where Saul Pickens used to live. Condos will rise from these old homesteads. My memories will be buried under concrete and double-paned windows and five-million-dollar views.

I climb faster.

When I first got here, Ma told me the condo people came by and plied her with a million-dollar offer. She told them to go to hell.

Blood is ringing in my ears. There's nothing to get angry about in the city; everything is glossed over. Here, it's rough around the edges, sharp and pointy like old people's feet. I don't look behind me. I don't want to look down the hill.

Ma stopped saying much day before yesterday. We've had a few visitors, people paying their last respects. No one's on this mountain anymore but Ma and a few others. When she dies, the mountain will rise up and consume her and the house, and condos will sprout from every ridge like weeds.

. . .

As death gets closer, Ma looks younger. Eyebrows arch, delicate and thin. The skin has translucence. She could have been a beauty in the city with money and the right clothes. No one got to see Ma's prettiness behind the dirty work boots and the hair, tied back hurriedly each morning before she did chores. We washed our hair once a week, and when I first went to the city, I thought it so strange all the water people used. How clean were we supposed to get? And what if you didn't look as clean as the person next to you or didn't have the right clothes?

There's a good thing I learned in the cities: how easy and warm some families can be. I want that, but all I have here is the harshness of winter coming, the tang of cold in the air, and the constant ring and roar of the yellow bulldozers. There won't be a person left who can remember Colby's guineas. The trees are gone, uprooted and thrown in a huge snaggly pile. I'm wishing for chickens like Colby had: reds and barred rocks, clucking and crooning. The bulldozer backs up, beeping, and throws more dirt.

We never thought twice about the five-mile walk, one way,

from the house to town, when I was little. Other mountain kids joined me on the way down, springing out of the woods like hiding animals, as if they'd slept there overnight. They're all gone now, off to the city. I wonder if their faces are like mine. I can't decide whether city or country is winning. Hard eyes, like my mother's, glitter with an animal danger. I'm beginning to remember the names of plants and trees.

It is never quiet until night when the dozers quit. I hike at night now, closing the creaky cabin door quietly as I can. I've learned to see in the dark. I know where every rock is, and I can find the path, even though there are no moon and stars. Foggy air winnows along the ground. I edge my left foot on a pointy rock, and I realize I'm not wearing my own running shoes. I threw on Ma's sneakers, old, thin ones she liked to wear in the garden because they had flat bottoms and didn't have all kinds of crevices that collected dirt. Our feet are the same size.

I'm scrambling up the steepest part of the mountain. There's a rock outcrop I haven't been to since I was a kid, and I used to sit here and look out over the holler. I'd look at the tops of those trees and know I could walk over these mountains. If I never had to go off the mountain again, that would have been okay. I could live, hunt, listen to the birds and the noises. Sometimes I'd hear the blood-curdling scream of one of the big cats; they sound like a woman being killed. I sit down on a rock.

Chill bores through my jeans. Rock is amazing, its ability to hold cold or heat. Wind brushes the edge of my eye. My feet are damp in the thin sneakers.

Crinkling rustles behind me, the rasp of dry leaves and the twiggy branches of a shrub. "You're back," whispers a child's voice.

"Sylvia?" There's a sweet ache in my chest.

"Don't turn around," she warns, but I can't stop. There is fog, twisting and curling from the dark of the ground, and a form, shifting. A child's voice, Sylvia's face, Ma's face, something between adult and child, and both.

"You're it," she says. "You are the mountain."

Cold oozes into my bones and breath. I inhale ice air. My lungs freeze; I can't speak. The fog dissipates, and there is nothing behind me—only the cold and shrubs and hollow quiet on the top of a mountain in the middle of a dark, lightless morning.

. . .

My feet know the way down. "Mountain sense," the people around here call it.

There's a low light in the cabin, and I wonder if Ma will have passed while I was gone. Ghosts come for ones that are crossing over. Sylvia died too young for Ma to push her away. All that remained was the never-ending work with the garden and the animals and hunting. I left to forget.

Ma's headboard has a shelf on it where a battery lamp sits, along with a book or two that haven't been touched in weeks. The lamp spills weak light onto her face. The quilt covers her chest, and it barely rises and falls. And I hear the water in her breath; trapped fog. I reach to turn off the light, but her eyes open and hold me.

My fingers tingle on the base of the lamp. The yeast smell is replaced with dusty porcelain, mint, rose.

Her eyes bore into my face.

She is holding me, telling stories that can't come from her mouth. The eyes are taking me in. I don't look away. The battery clock on the wall ticks in endless rotation.

I reach under the quilt and take her hand. There is no strength there. Her eyes hold me, expanding, contracting more than the mountains, only a woman's eyes: my Ma.

Her hand is still. I squeeze. She stares, drinking me. Her fingers are blue. We never have enough until the door is almost shut. Then we know it will end; that it will have to be enough. She's giving me what she can; she knows the door is shutting.

"Ma," I whisper, "I saw Sylvia in the woods on the top of the mountain."

I feel the heat from her eyes and her hand, even though her hand is cold.

Her eyes drift from mine and go within. She stares at nothing. Ma's eyes half close. The quilt is still, and the water in Ma's chest ceases its movement. A gray edge of light lines the eastern horizon.

. . .

I bury Ma in the old hills tradition. I wash her body and smooth her legs, marveling at the tiny ankles. I massage her cheeks and put silver coins over her eyes so the spirits can't crawl into her empty body. I dress her in the best clothes of hers I can find. Her spirit takes its time. She doesn't want to leave the mountain.

Jim Feeny builds a coffin, and we bury her in the town cemetery. We all dig the grave: me, Jim, and the others Ma knew who are still here and still alive.

. . .

The mountains come through my pores. There's dirt outside to be worked for a garden. In this cabin, every wall has memories. The table where we ate, Ma and I and Sylvia and Daddy, until Sylvia died and he disappeared. And then Ma got hard.

Until the end.

I'm eating oatmeal, the rolled oats kind that Ma bought from the general store in town. We used to trade goat milk and rabbit meat for eggs and flour and oatmeal. No one used money because no one had any.

I don't know if I can go back to the city.

My Escort doesn't belong here. I need a dusty, rough car that can take rocks flying up from the road and nicking its paint. I need my feet.

. . .

The bulldozer is backing up, then forward, back, forward. *Beep beep beep, roar. Beep beep, roar.* The land is under my fingers. The cold of the mountains settles in my bones. The fog is thick with ghosts and memories, and I may see the tendrils of Ma and Sylvia rise up from the ground and speak with quiet. The cabin needs painting, and I need to put a garden in. When the bulldozers stop roaring and the condos are up, I'll plant trees in front of the porch windows so I don't have to see the valley, or I'll shut the porch for good, or I'll stare at the holler in the way mountain people do, in the way my mother did as she died, and I'll drink it in. I'll keep chickens and remember Colby and his wine and eggs and screeching guineas. And the rooster that attacked kids when we walked past his land. I'll remember the mountain because it is still here, among the condos, for those who know to see.

the last great chance

Bardy thought he'd never seen anything so idiotic. He looked through unfocused eyes at the circular UFO that sat in his back yard.

"What the . . ." His head throbbed with the force of his hangover. *Musta been one helluva party last night . . . me, myself, and I . . .*

Why wasn't he in bed? It came to him, gradual clarity through a heavy fog. Every thought hurt like the force of a thousand knives: *floor, patio door, my trailer house. Did I sleep on the floor? Who cares? Me, myself, and I.* He giggled, then grimaced at the pain of hearing his own voice.

Must get upright. Water on face. Coffee. Slowly, he went through the motions, trying to ignore the nausea that churned in his gut. If he could just get through the next two hours, he would start feeling better. Hangover Road. He'd been there many times before.

But when he returned to his patio door and looked out at his back yard in the boonies, the silver UFO still sat gleaming in the early eastern sunlight.

For seven days and seven nights, Bardy stared at the UFO. He didn't go outside and didn't call anyone. Not unusual, considering his lifestyle. Guys around town knew Bardy as a loner. He rarely drove into town in his beat-up truck. The truck looked like he lived in it. Tourists passing through the small town got nervous if they saw him, a rough-looking man with a dazed, hermit-like look in his eyes. He dressed like the poorest of poor and lived on the edge, barely eating but making sure his alcohol supply didn't run out.

Drinking banished the ghosts. Alcohol cut through the haze of the phantoms that plagued him every hour of day and night.

Alcohol might be able to banish the ghosts, but it didn't do a damn thing to the silver UFO in his yard.

Bardy tried different combinations. He drank in the morning and stopped at night. He drank at night and stopped in the morning. He drank all the time. At the end of seven days, he was wasted, shaky, feeling nearer to death than he'd ever been. His throat felt like a thousand molten ramrods had been shoved deep into its soft flesh, jostled back and forth by a laughing devil. The silver thing looked at home in his yard, surrounded by the spruce and the swamp and the hatching mosquitoes.

On the eighth day, relatively hangover free, Bardy ventured out. The trailer home wobbled as he tried to open the sliding patio door as quietly as possible. Wouldn't do to shake up whatever was in there.

The thing stood about a hundred feet from his door. He looked at it. *Now what?*

Bardy had never in his life given UFOs a second thought. Prickles of apprehension raced through his veins. He walked up to the thing, one step at time, trying to ignore the quivering in his legs.

Before he could talk himself out of it, he raised his hand in a fist and knocked.

Cold metal.

Bardy waited for some noise, a response, vaporization.

He knocked again.

Silence. Only the faint sound of the wind blowing through the spruce and tamarack.

He stared at the thing, and his body turned to jelly with the after-effects of adrenaline. When he could walk again, Bardy turned back to his house, went in, and pondered. An idea took root in his head.

. . .

"Mr. Mayor, this is our chance to make the town some money. You're always wanting to put the town on the map. Bring in more money from the tourists. Talking about economic development."

The six-member city council looked at the disheveled man, their eyes half shut in a bland expression.

"I read the paper," Bardy said, a trace of defensiveness in his voice. "I got something here to offer. Logging and mining ain't gonna last forever."

The mayor gave Bardy a cold look. "Let me get this right. You say there's a UFO in your back yard."

"Yep."

"And you propose we make the city a ton of money by charging admission to see this so-called landmark?"

Bardy nodded. "'Course," he added, "We split the proceeds fifty-fifty."

"'Course." The mayor's voice held an edge of sarcasm, but Bardy didn't care. He had the thing in his back yard. They didn't. Maybe he could get rich as a lottery winner. No more worrying and scrimping. Plenty to drink.

"I dunno." Another council member spoke up. "It could be risky. Aren't we endangering lives? How do we know whatever's in there isn't hostile? Maybe we should call in the government."

"Screw the government," someone muttered.

Bardy grinned. A typical sentiment around here.

"Consider the source of the information." A council member looked straight through Bardy. "The guy's a drunk. Maybe he's hallucinating. How do we know this thing's for real?"

Silence. Bardy restrained himself from jumping in. *Let them figure it out.* He watched them fidget, look at him, and look away.

"What would it hurt?" A council member shrugged.

"I guess we could take a trip," said the mayor.

.   .   .

Bardy paced his trailer house, oblivious to the reverberations he sent through the thin structure. *Cheap-ass construction.* They'd be here any minute, the mayor and his council members. He might like a drink now and then, but he sure as hell wasn't crazy. That thing sat in his yard, and they were going to see it. Then they could all talk about ideas for economic development.

He stared out the window. The UFO threw silver shadows in the sunlight. Bardy never found the nerve to go out again and knock on the cold exterior. He stayed in his house, venturing out only to drive into town for the occasional errand. For as much respect as he had for the thing, he feared it. The little green men could reach out and grab him at any time. They might take him from his bed into the cold, hard, insides of that thing. Why call them men? Maybe they couldn't ever be sensed or seen in a normal human way. Maybe they prowled his house at this moment, observing him and snickering. It gave him the creeps.

"Anybody home?"

Bardy jumped, his skin tingling. When he'd recovered his composure, he opened the front door.

The six-member council piled into his small living room. When was the last time he'd had this many people here?

"So where's this thing?" Gerald Petersen spoke, overweight and huffy, the owner of an auto repair business.

"Didn't ya see it?"

"Nope."

Bardy scratched his head, noticing where the hair was

beginning to thin near the top of his scalp. One day he'd be par-tially bald like his father. They should have glimpsed the UFO around the side of the trailer, even coming in the front door. Maybe they'd been afraid to look at the thing without the protec-tion of the house around them.

"Come on over here." He pointed to the sliding glass door, cur-tains drawn shut for dramatic effect. "Here's a good view." The verti-cal shades rattled and swung as he pulled them open. "Ta da!"

Silence.

The mayor stared at the back yard. "You dragged me out here to see this?"

"Huh?" Panic began to climb behind Bardy's eyes. "Don't you see it? Don't you see it?" Dimly, he heard his voice rising like a train whistle.

"I see a back yard that's had better days. How long's it been since you been to the dump?" The mayor pointed at several dozen bags of trash, thrown in a pile to one side where the mowed grass ended and the swamp vegetation began.

"Hey, I can't afford the damned dump prices. Don't you see it?" Bardy's heart hurled toward a bottomless hole, and his stom-ach rode up his torso into his throat.

"I see it," whispered Gerald. He heaved with the effort of speaking, and Bardy saw the beads of sweat on Gerald's upper lip. "Oh my God! It's there."

. . .

The next city council meeting was packed with the biggest crowd in the history of the town. The mayor looked out at his townspeople. These sheep showed up for an Oprah-like rumor of flying saucers in back yards, but where were they when something important needed discussing? They'd let the council make some decision about taxes or road repair and then bitch about it later. He sighed. *This'll be the last time I'll run for mayor, God willing,* he thought.

"Let's get this meeting started," he called.

Two hours later, they were still going at it. The mayor's head was beginning to spin. The people who could see the thing wanted to charge admission to tourists, put the town on the map. The people who couldn't see the thing thought the rest of them were insane. Many had never bothered to visit Bardy's dump of a property to try to see the UFO. Some residents objected to a steady stream of traffic through town. Why push progress? Life was good here.

"Just 'cause you can't see it don't mean it ain't there!" yelled Gerald, his face flushed with zeal. "I saw it, man. I saw it. How do you know they ain't watching us right now, laughing at us?"

Something to think about, pondered the mayor. How in heck was he supposed to bring this problem to any sort of closure when half the people could see the thing and half couldn't?

Another hour later, with the townspeople still arguing and nothing accomplished, the mayor thought Gerald's supposition might be pretty accurate.

. . .

Bardy left the meeting with a new resolve. *To hell with them all.* On his land, he could proceed any damned way he liked. He constructed a sign at the end of his driveway: "Ten Dollars! See the UFO or your money back!"

Risky, he knew. He trembled with the chance he was taking until he realized he had nothing to lose. If nobody saw the UFO, he had nowhere to go, did he? Bardy'd be back where he'd started. And if they did—

They did. The cars soon stretched down Bardy's dead-end dirt road. Every one of the people walked away smiling.

"I knew them things was true," said an old man with yellowed teeth, one of them missing in the front. Slobber hung between the surrounding teeth when the man talked. "I dreamed about them since I was a kid."

Bardy nodded. He was glad he could make his customers happy, and he was raking in the bucks. First, there were twenty cars a day, then fifty, and then a hundred. They came from further and further away. They came from Duluth, from the Twin Cities. People came from the next state over. People came from several states away. There were families with folding chairs and screaming kids; old women and men who claimed they had to see this sight before they died; yuppies in SUVs who walked away with a dazed look, the tension dropping from their faces like melting butter. Bardy had one rule: a five-minute limit per car. He had to keep traffic moving. The rest of them waited on the road. Most were content to look at the UFO. One or two knocked on the exterior as Bardy had done. No response.

Bardy had so much cash he didn't know what to do with it all. He also had no time to drink. He found himself thinking clearly for the first time in years. After several shaky days, he had an astonishing revelation: *I don't miss the stuff.*

He smiled out the window at the UFO. It gleamed in the moonlight, throwing strange shadows around in the swamp grass. That mystery made a lot of things very, very possible.

.   .   .

RAP RAP!

"Viewing hours are over," muttered Bardy. Who in hell would be knocking at his door this late at night?

RAP!

Reluctantly, he pulled himself away from the TV. Leno came in pretty good on his new big-screen. Bardy almost felt like he was right in the studio, and the state-of-the-art stereo system enhanced the sound from the show. Bardy clapped along with the audience when Jay made a funny joke. Sighing, he muted the volume. *This had better be good at eleven p.m.*

The force of the light pushed him off his feet when he opened the door. He flew backwards, landing on his ass. Bardy's limbs shook uncontrollably. When he dared, he looked up, putting his hand up to his forehead to try and see something past the light.

"What'd you expect? Little green men?" He heard the mocking voice in his brain even though he could not see whatever spoke.

"What are you?" The words wobbled, rattling like marbles from the trembling of his lips.

"You know what we are, Bardy. But do you know what you are?"

Scared. Ready to piss in my pants. For the first time in weeks, Bardy longed for a drink. The light in the doorway blinded him, and he could make out nothing beyond it.

"You are incapable of perceiving us in our correct form. Be glad of it."

"You're reading my mind." Bardy felt an insane urge to smash his head against the cheap trailer walls, hoping this bad scene would go away.

"Forget it. You're our emissary. You have a job."

Bardy whimpered. "Please. I don't want to be an emissary." He had no idea what the word meant but figured it had something to do with responsibility and the strange and scary light thing at his door.

"Light thing?" Again the scorn, tinged with incredulity. "You humans are barbarians. You kill each other, ruin your planet, commit great evil in the name of your gods. It's amazing you're still alive."

Bardy shook. This was worse than the DTs, worse than the strongest, strangest hangover he could remember in his drinking life. And it was too clear. It wasn't going to go away. "Why are you here?" he dared in a hesitant whisper. "Why are you bothering me?"

"You tremble, and you should. This is a test. Don't take it personally," the voice reassured. Bardy could almost sense the thing in his mind looking around at his shabby trailer, taking in the card

THE LAST GREAT CHANCE

table where he ate meals on, the second-hand sofa with the cigarette burns. "Circumstances led us to your quiet area of the world. You're it."

Bardy didn't like the sound of that. He wished the damn thing had never landed in his yard, wished he could give all the money that he didn't know how to spend back to the hoards that had come and gaped at its silver shadows.

"You have a big problem. Can humans cooperate? Some of them see our transport, and some of them don't. Why?"

"Damned if I know." Bardy stood up and took a trembling step backward from the blinding light.

"Sit down!" The command boomed in Bardy's head, and he turned into a blubbering terror. He slumped to the floor, legs like jelly.

"They've lost the ability to transcend, to believe in the fantastic, the 'more', the something that is not part of reality as they perceive it. They've lost what you call magic. Do you know what this means?"

Bardy shook his head, wanting desperately to blow his nose but not daring to turn away and find a tissue.

"They can't go on."

Bardy looked around, noticed the gray wallboard near the door, and wished he was back in front of the mutely moving picture on the big screen. Leno was probably over by now.

"If humans can't transcend to admit the existence of magic—that's it."

"Huh?" Bardy felt the cold mercury of finality in his heart, like the day he'd put his dog down. His chest was ice, the walls of his heart brittle.

"This is your last chance. If humans can believe in the existence of something beyond their reality, your world gets to continue. If not—"

"What kind of crap is that?" The ice around Bardy's heart shattered into a thousand pieces, moving with fear.

"That's it."

"Who says?"

"Powers above all of us. Humankind's chance. Right here in your own back yard." Bardy thought he heard the slight mocking. "It's up to you. Get your people to see the magic, to go beyond what they know. You have one week in your time."

"But what if—"

"One week."

Bardy shut his eyes against the burning glare of the light. When he dared look again, the doorway stood empty, open, waiting.

.   .   .

He groaned and rolled over. His back was sore. Through his head ran an old song from the 1970s, something about the power of magic. Bardy opened his eyes. He must have fallen asleep on the floor. In front of him, the wobbly front door hung open, letting in mosquitoes.

He had work to do!

One week. One week to convince everyone he knew about magic?? What the hell kind of deal was that? Or what? The end of the Earth? Of all humankind? It didn't seem fair.

There was no time to think. He had to act. Bardy threw on clothes, some from the dirty pile on the floor, some from the dresser drawer, probably clean. When had he done laundry last? Time moved too quickly. He pushed his feet into work boots, forgetting to lace them, and stumbled out the door, heading for the truck. Fast food wrappers were scattered on the seat. Bardy pushed them over to the passenger side. Discovering food again had been nice. He'd even put on a little badly needed weight.

By the time he drove into town, Bardy's head pounded with inadequacy. What the hell had he planned on doing here? Where was he supposed to start? Why did he, of all people, have to be the emissary, or whatever the word was?

THE LAST GREAT CHANCE

One week. One week.

The words of the . . . thing . . . he'd talked with droned through his head, a laser beam in a sea of confusion. *Humans' last chance. Can't go on. Believe in magic.*

"You're so stupid." The voice of his father mocked him, blending with his own thoughts until he wasn't sure who spoke.

Bardy swerved violently to avoid missing a telephone pole. He pulled over, shaking and unable to drive. No one seemed to be around.

He looked to the right and realized he sat on the shoulder of one of the town's two main roads. Ahead of him was the town pharmacy.

Bardy jumped out of the truck, slamming the driver's door that groaned with the protest of rusty hinges. But the glass door to the pharmacy stood unyielding as ice, locked on the one day it closed for business: Sunday.

Church!

Morning, it had to be morning. Bardy snapped his neck up to look at the sky, feeling a strange pain shoot through his arm. Where was a clock when you needed one? The sun hung in the eastern horizon, promising possible church services. Before his gut got the better of him, he gunned the truck toward the biggest church in town.

The glass door hissed as Bardy threw it open. A formal usher automatically reached out to give Bardy a program, then recoiled in horror at the sight of the unkempt man with stringy blonde hair that hung past his shoulders. Bardy's eyes glittered with primitive wildness as he pushed his way into the main church area. Boot laces flying, unmatched socks, and a burger wrapper sticking out of one coverall pocket, he barged down the center aisle as parishioners turned around to identify the storm in their calm. The priest gaped at the apparition coming his way.

"Call the cops," the priest muttered to one of the altar boys.

"Magic! We've got to believe in magic!" Bardy stepped up to

the altar, a man with a mission. *What…what were the words of the light thing?* It jumbled in Bardy's head. He had to make sure the right words got out. One week.

"Got to believe!" he cried out. "Believe in the unreal. Or—" The words! He had to get the words. "Or it's the end for humans. That's it. That's it!" He screamed the repetition, hoping that maybe, just maybe, the urgency would sink into the people in front of him. But they sat stiff as boards, expressions of politeness, shock, distaste, scorn, flickering like ambulance lights across their faces.

"You are disrupting my service." The priest spoke slowly and deliberately, the words mouthed as if to a deaf child. "Get out of here now, or the police will take you away."

Bardy ignored the fleshy man in robes. Hadn't this priest been one of the people who couldn't see the UFO?

"You must believe in magic!" he cried. "They told me so!"

"We believe in God," said the priest, every syllable caked with the deliberateness of centuries.

"No, no, they told me so, or it's the end for humans. Please! Please!"

Why did the feelings of inadequacy come all his life? Why now when he needed to make a difference? He was a rock, pulled back into the ocean by a strong undertow. His mother shoved him there, his father flung the stone into the tides, and the booze had let him enjoy the depths of a watery existence until now.

"Please," he cried. "It's the end." He barely noticed the strong male hands that grabbed him around his upper arm, leading him stumbling out of the church.

.   .   .

"Congratulations, pal. You did it."

Was Bardy sober? Lately, things had been so crazy he'd felt drunk without taking a drink. He opened his eyelids. *Careful, careful.* He crashed his forearm across his face to cover his eyes before he had time to think about the reflex.

The light things. Two of them talking to him. When did it all end?

"It's over."

Slowly, he put his arm down. He could not look directly at the light but turned to note his surroundings. Gleaming and circular, metallic looking. "I'm inside?"

"Yes. You and others who believed."

He took it in, eyes focusing for the first time. The shape appeared quite small, yet also huge. *Impossible. How could it be both?* And many people surrounded him. He recognized a few: Gerald and the old man with slobber between his teeth.

"Poor humans," said one of the light things. Bardy could swear it almost made a sympathetic noise. "They failed their first multiple reality test."

"Well, most of them, except these lucky few."

"Where we going?" asked Bardy. Did he really want to know?

"Well, my friend, you and your peers passed the multiple reality test. You were able to believe in a reality beyond your experience, so you can go wherever you want—whatever reality you want."

"Really?" Bardy's thoughts fell into place before he could catalogue or recall them, before he could stop.

• • •

The swamp trees danced with a wind from the west. Bardy loved watching the storm come in. He looked out the back of the trailer, feeling adequate for the first time in his life. He was seamless, ageless, memoryless. Bardy needed no one, no crutch, so great grew the inner strength within him. He thought about booze no longer, and the rare memory of bourbon or a beer set his stomach on edge. He had no recollection of childhood or most of the past, an arrangement that suited him fine. A swarm of purple martins dive-bombed the yard, feasting with a frenetic urge on mosquitoes. Two landed and mated in a burned out, circular indentation in the grass.

crossroads

amned if this walking-between-the-worlds crap didn't follow me into the afterlife.

I spend my whole life trying to walk the red road in a white world. I can't wait to die and go to the *Anishinabe* Otherworld. I'm in for a big surprise.

When I cross over, I'm standing on two roads, one foot in each. The *Anishinabe* Otherworld is on my left: ricing canoes, the maple sugar camps, the spirits.

On my right, a huge government agency: the Bureau of Indian Affairs.

I see the bureaucrats in white shirts doling out the money. I'm a ghost, and I have no physical body, but I can feel what must be my feet, firmly planted in each world. I blink with eyes that are only a memory, rub my forehead with hands that are only an idea, trying to absorb the idea of the white-shirts here. White men. *Chimooks*.

Howah. The BIA *in the afterlife? How much weirder can it get?*

. . .

I think it all started for me when Father Stone began coming onto the rez. Actually, it started long before that for my people, the *Anishinabe*, the Ojibwe. Father Stone would drive up to our rez in his 1950s Mercury on Sunday mornings. I'd never seen a car like that, the kind with the rear window that went up and down. Auntie Lacey had an old Ford truck, but it was half sunk in the swamp behind her cabin, and there it sat, the rust eating it away. There weren't many other cars on the rez; most of them were broken down or ran like a giant chainsaw. We never knew when Father Stone's car was coming over the hill because it was so quiet.

Father Stone drove sixty-seven miles from the nearest off-rez town, north on the spruce- and swamp-lined two-lane county road that dissected the rez. He was doing his damndest to snatch up as many rez kids as he could and save their souls. The man would have gotten down on his hands and knees and dug the foundation for a church on the reservation, had he the means. I could see the wheels working in his mind even though I was only a seven-year-old boy; even though I never liked his face with the narrow nose, sharp eyes, and reddish hair.

To bribe us kids to come to church, he organized trips to the city—a day at a theme park, a baseball game, a basketball game. But if you wanted to go on those excursions, you had to go to church. All year. Every Sunday at eight a.m., like clockwork, we could expect him.

When I was seven, Father Stone showed up for the first time on a Wednesday afternoon. "*Boozhoo*," he greeted us in broken Ojibwe, walking in our cabin as if he owned it.

Auntie Lacey, who raised me and my brothers, hardly gave him a second look. She was doing the dishes in the kitchen, which was really part of the rest of the house, a one-room cabin. I could hear the Mercury running outside, an audible testament to Father Stone's confidence in his evangelical techniques.

"Ready for church?" he asked, with the exaggerated smile of a man who was uncomfortable around children.

"I don't want to go."

It was warm for March, and I wanted to be outside, throwing stones at squirrels, tromping through the swamp before it got too wet and buggy to walk in, smearing Petey with dirty snow. I hated Father Stone's somber church with its high dark ceilings that shut out the world. I hated the plodding organ music and the words everyone said and sang together in droning, bored tones.

Father Stone ignored my comment. "Did you fast today?"

Auntie Lacey stiffened, and let out a little snort of laughter. She turned toward us from her dishes. "Jimmy's too young to do a vision quest."

"Vision quest, vision quest," I whispered to taunt the priest.

Auntie Lacey glared at me. Father Stone looked uncomfortable and fidgeted with one foot, swiveling his heel back and forth.

"I don't want to go," I repeated. I'd give up the basketball games.

"Get in the car," Auntie Lacey muttered. A crucifix hung above the old white sink where she worked.

Father Stone put a meaty hand on my shoulder and steered me out the door. Already I could see Al, Petey, and Stevie squeezed in the back seat where I'd join them. Father Stone could stuff at least two more kids in the front. None of my friends looked any happier than I was. I thought about the church and how much it reminded me of a dreary cave. I looked at the road we were driving on. That night, I dreamed of two roads: one white, the other red. They ran together, diverged, ran together again.

. . .

It's cold in the Otherworld.

Everything feels so unfocused. I can't move on. I'm still rooted in two places, each foot on a different road.

I worked hard to get here after I died, after my body sat for three days and the living relations honored me with healing food to send my spirit off on a safe journey. They set small paper plates of blueberries, maple sugar, wild rice, and venison next to me as my spirit made ready to leave the body.

Released as spirit, I crossed a great river to get here. *What will it be like,* I wondered, *to live in a world where I can finally fit, where I can walk one road? How will it feel?* I'd be in real Indian Country.

The river was wide, and I was tired as I swam across it. Only the thought of the waiting Otherworld kept me going. Everyone knows the journey to the Otherworld is difficult, but it never occurred to me to doubt what might be there when I finally crossed over.

I'd see shallow lakes full of wild rice; *manoomin.* The *manoomin* would grow so thick you could hardly see the canoes through the waving brown stems as my people traveled, two to a boat, one poling and the other knocking the rice into the canoe with tapered cedar sticks. The Otherworld reminded me of times when we kept the rice for ourselves. It was enough to get us through the winter. There were times when we didn't sell the sacred *manoomin,* not even to our tribal council. Instead, we hunted. There were those times when we all knew our traditions and spoke our own language. I looked forward to greeting my relatives and people from my tribe who had already crossed over.

When I finally dragged myself from the river, shivering with the ghost water and chilled by the Otherworldly winds, I couldn't breathe.

The People to the left were beckoning. It was all maddening— so maddening that I couldn't seem to move.

Bureaucrats were to the right: meetings, clocks, and a figure in white robes. Why should I be surprised to see Father Stone? He had crossed over twenty years before me, and he was the first one to firmly brand me with vestiges of the white world.

• • •

The Mercury bumped eastward down the county road toward Father Stone's church. We were still on the rez portion of the road, and that year's potholes and frost heaves were beginning to push through the concrete, leftovers from our long winter. A black rosary hung from the rearview mirror, swinging as we hit another pothole. Then, with a suddenness that reminded me of the way Father Stone slammed his Bible shut at the end of a sermon, the road smoothed out, and the rosary swung a little less. We were off the rez, on the portion of road that'd been patched and repaved in the last five years.

"Children, tonight is a very special night. Do you know what tonight's Mass symbolizes?"

The nuns had drummed it into our heads a thousand times, but I wasn't going to give him the satisfaction of my response. I looked down, staring at the floor mats that were dirty with months of grit dragged into this car on the snowy feet of reluctant children. We were all silent.

"*Banung*," muttered Stevie. He made his index finger into the shape of a limp penis. Ojibwe slang.

Father Stone gave us a sharp look in the mirror. We giggled.

"Big *banung*," growled Petey, and we laughed harder.

Father Stone cleared his voice. "Today is Ash Wednesday, the day you acknowledge that you belong to Jesus."

When we arrived in town, Father Stone pulled up to the door of the church. Sister Cecelia made sure we each stopped at the holy water fount, and we dipped our fingers into the water and made the sign of the cross before we walked down the aisle. Most of the people in town were in church; their stares bored into my back. There was a reserved pew in the front just for us kids.

Later in the Mass, Father Stone branded each of us with the ashes of last year's Easter palms, making the sign of the cross on our foreheads. Hours later, years later, every day of my life, I felt the determined, precise movement of his fingers.

I dreamed of two roads that crossed…and went nowhere.

. . .

My feet stay planted in both worlds. I try to pick up each foot but can't. I can't go completely into one world or another.

On my right, a bureaucrat in a white shirt and tie approaches me.

Father Stone remains in the background, with the patience of eternity written on his face. I think that's the part of his presence that most unnerves me. Over his years of dealing with skins, he's learned to be as patient as we are.

The bureaucrat is a skin in white man's clothes: an Apple. Red on the outside, white on the inside. I don't recognize him. He looks at his watch. "Meeting at two p.m.," he says. "That's in a half an hour."

I've learned to wait; it's a survival mechanism. I make my face blank. Apple knows what I'm doing; I see him stifle a look of exasperation.

A fat *Chimook* in a white shirt walks over beside him.

"Why do I need to go to a meeting?" I keep my voice soft and expressionless. "Let me go on to the *Anishinabe* Otherworld."

"Not until we've determined your blood quantum," says Apple, "and your income level and your land ownership."

Money? Blood quantum? Land ownership? What kind of corrupted Otherworld is this?

"Wait." I hear Auntie Lacey breathe into my ear, a ghost of a memory.

After several seconds, Apple and *Chimook* move away.

"Those people," *Chimook* mutters. "You never know what they're thinking."

. . .

I practiced a religion of survival as I grew older, a blended necessity of Catholic superstitions and Native traditions. I grew so used to it after a while that the hybrid mixture of red and white beliefs felt like a second skin. Much of it I learned from Auntie Lacey. She went to Mass whenever she could get a ride. She ran her fingers over her plastic rosary, saying Hail Marys on each touch of a bead. Dream catchers hung in the house, even though Father Stone looked askance at them when he visited. Auntie Lacey made a jingle dress for a niece, even though she wouldn't dance in the powwows herself for religious reasons.

Jesus worked his way into my life, but I made him my own.

I stroked the beads of the rosary, and the glitter of the tiny crucifix caught my eye. But instead of muttering Hail Marys, I repeated the Ojibwe words I knew, using a soft voice and muffling the consonants so the nuns wouldn't overhear me and rap my fingers with a ruler. They didn't like it when we spoke our language. "*Mii gwetch*," I whispered. "*Mii gwetch.* Thank you."

The nuns showed us pictures of a pale Christ with thin hair that came to his shoulders and a short beard. But my Christ had brown skin and no hint of a beard. My Christ talked to me in Ojibwe. He laughed and told dirty jokes like Auntie Lacey, like Petey's granddad. Father Stone watched me doing my Sunday school lessons. I smiled to myself, enlivening the stories with my own characters.

"Christ listens to you, doesn't he?" asked Father Stone. I could see the warmth in the priest's eyes, could almost imagine this priest cared about me.

I nodded, but I put a hood over my eyes so the priest couldn't see into my soul. I didn't think Father Stone would care for an Indian Christ.

. . .

At two p.m. in the Otherworld, I can see the bureaucrats looking at their watches: Apple and *Chimook*. My feet are still on two roads, though the pull is stronger in the white-shirt direction. The white world is closer with its conference tables and filing cabinets and clocks. The People are farther away. Auntie Lacey is waving at me, but she's smaller. I hear her tell me to wait.

The white shirts are clearing their throats and giving me pointed looks. I ignore them. I make my face blank.

What can they do? They can't do anything until I decide to cooperate. I could stand here forever in stasis, one foot in each world, driving them crazy for eternity, but I want to get onto the Anishinabe Otherworld.

They look at their watches. Finally I look up, signaling with my eyes that I'm ready to talk.

Chimook looks particularly crabby. "Do you realize what time it is?" He's red around the neck.

Apple has a bland expression on his face, as if he can't decide to be mad or not.

"It's almost eight p.m." *Chimook* can't keep the irritation out of his voice.

Father Stone is still in the background, behind the bureaucrats. He's waiting his turn.

I smile at *Chimook* and Apple. "Indian time," I say.

.   .   .

The meeting drags on, reminding me of the things I can't forget. Father Stone's cross of ash throbs on my forehead, and I'm a seven-year-old boy again. It could have happened yesterday or a minute ago or whatever meaning time has in this Otherworld.

Chimook shuffles some papers and clears his throat. We're sitting at a nondescript table, even though I'm still in two worlds. It could be any office in America.

In the later years of my own term as tribal chairman, even our rez started to look this way during my lifetime, I think, with a pang of guilt. What could I do? White ways crept in. It was impossible to lead a tribal council, to carry out any sort of administration without incorporating meetings, deadlines, grants for government money: BIA money from that bastard, hybrid, necessary organization.

"We've already established that you have appropriate blood quantum to move on to the *Anishinabe* Otherworld," says *Chimook.*

Apple nods. "One-fourth Ojibwe, from your mother's mother."

I grin, breaking the non-expression on my face. There's always time for a joke.

"Yes, Apple," I say, "but do you have enough blood quantum to move on?"

Apple looks embarrassed, and I see the blush on his red skin. He's forgotten how to have fun, spent too much time with *Chimook.* "I'm not moving on for now," he mutters.

Chimook makes two neat piles of paper in front of him, taking the blood quantum paperwork and turning it over in the second pile, straightening both again. It's quiet until I hear the rustling of robes.

Father Stone is standing closer, his sharp eyes glaring at me with none of the rheumy quality of the old. His hair is still red; it never grayed as he aged. His smiles are still forced.

Howah. If only the river to the Otherworld had washed the ashes away for good. Their physical evidence, an oily smear on my forehead, is long gone. I ran out of the church on that long-ago Ash Wednesday service, flinging my hand into the first source of water I could find, the holy water fount. I cupped my hand in the water, splashing it all over my forehead, rubbing my skin until I thought the ashes were gone.

It didn't matter. The cross remains branded on my forehead, the stamp of Father Stone's Christ, impossible to remove. During my life it throbbed when I woke up, it dragged me off the red road, it invaded my dreams with its precise conclusions, it haunts me now in the Otherworld.

. . .

Chimook speaks. "There's the issue of land ownership."

Sha. Can't he be more original? I'm silent for a long time.

Chimook begins to look uncomfortable, fidgeting, swiveling in the ergonomic office chair.

Finally, I speak. "What's the issue?"

Apple pulls out a map of the rez, laying it flat on the table. He smoothes it, letting his red fingers glide to one of the boundaries, the place where my land abuts. I notice for the first time that Apple wears a ring with a thick gold band and a square onyx stone, a tiny diamond embedded in the center.

"The reservation boundaries have recently changed," says Apple. He doesn't look at me.

"Seems there was a misinterpretation of the treaty," says *Chimook*, picking up on Apple's discomfort.

"*Howah!*" I snort. "Ain't that the truth!"

Apple looks at the table, refusing to meet my eyes.

"One fourth of one of your ten acres now falls outside the reservation boundaries," says *Chimook*. "You owe taxes for the last year."

"But that's the ceded territory!" I almost cry out.

Steady. "Wait," I hear Auntie Lacey say in the back of my head. *"Outwait them."*

I take a breath. "We have rights on the ceded territory. It's off-rez land, and the Treaty of 1854 gives us the right to harvest game from it in a traditional fashion."

"Let's see." *Chimook* pulls a calculator out of his pocket, his stomach straining against his white shirt. Sweat beads on his forehead with the effort of moving. "Hmm...998 times ten, for a total of $99.80." He hands me a property tax bill.

"White man," I say gently, "I brought no money with me into the Otherworld. Let it go. It's meaningless. Land can't be owned."

Chimook continues to stare at me, the piece of paper in front of him, his fingers on the top holding it in place. I think of my people, of Auntie Lacey, of the timeless cycle of moons and the wild rice harvest and the progression of the seasons.

I am not dreaming, but the roads are still in my mind. They are suspended; waiting, traveling nowhere, neither converging nor diverging, neither crossing nor dead-ending.

. . .

About a year later, *Chimook* and Apple get up from the table, taking their papers and admitting defeat. They leave.

I know it's been that long because I watched The People down the red road on my left. It gave me hope. I heard the voices of the *Anishinabe*, celebrating our traditions, unhindered by a white world.

We told stories in the winter, eating from caches of venison and wild rice. When spring came, we danced at the Time of the Bursting Bud Powwow, *Saa Gi Ba Gaa*. The syrup began to run from the maples, and we collected it, boiling it down. There were blueberries in the summer, and duck hunting and deer hunting and the wild rice harvest in late summer. We danced at *Miigwetch Manoomin* to give thanks for the wild rice.

I heard the voices of the people; I felt the road that holds us together as a tribe. It gave me patience and strength.

"*Mii gwetch*," I whisper to the Great Spirit.

. . .

The table has faded away. No clocks mark the passage of time, no calculators tabulate past-due amounts, no maps designate boundaries on land that can't be owned.

But the ashes on a seven-year-old's forehead still burn deeply in my mind, a pair of irreconcilable, crossed roads. My feet are still rooted; one on a white road, one on a red road.

Father Stone moves closer. He wears the robes of purple, the Easter colors. Determination gleams in his eyes. The ghost glyph, that ancient ash cross, throbs with the urgency of the present, not sixty-some years past.

"You always were a stubborn one," he says, and I can't tell whether his tone holds admiration or frustration or both. "Sister Cecilia nearly had a heart attack when you used the holy water to wash off your ashes."

"I knew my mind." It's a statement of fact more than pride. "I never asked to be adopted by your Jesus." But the words sound hesitant, not completely true. I knew my mind when I was seven. I had the stubbornness and clarity of a child. Things got muddier as I got older and made compromises. I wonder if this priest and his religion were the beginning of it.

I glare at him, the first real expression I've allowed on my face since I got to the Otherworld. This man stands between me and the People.

He smiles. "You don't want to go there, do you?" He looks toward the red road. "You can have something better—salvation."

"I can't wash this cross off. I still carry around your brand. I can't walk down the red road. What kind of magic do you hold, Ghost Priest?" He's an ordinary man by outward appearances, as nondescript as our own medicine man.

"Take your brand away," I plead. I want to stop seeing the crossed, irreconcilable roads. I want to untangle the hybrid mess that mixes the red and white worlds. I need the clarity of that seven-year-old. But Father Stone leans toward me, pulling me in with his eyes. I feel the white road becoming more focused.

"Only one road leads to Christ," Father Stone says.

"No," whispers Auntie Lacey. I turn toward the red road, and she's suddenly much closer, though not as close as the priest is. A silver crucifix glitters sharply from the rosary around her neck, but she's dim and blurry.

Father Stone's eyes glow with the passion that followed him into death. "Come with me." The tenderness in his voice scares me. "Know salvation, know joy." He's afraid for my demise.

But I think of seeing the People again, living the way we did before we had to walk two worlds. "I can't have my traditions on your white road. What kind of way is that to live? I waited all my life to meet my people here, to have our ways again, to not have to walk on two roads."

"Your road is the road to damnation!" hisses the priest. Then his tone turns cajoling. "There is only one way to Christ, one road to salvation."

"No...wait," whispers Auntie Lacey.

Out of the corner of my eye, I look at the People down the red road, and it tears my heart. I can't bear the thought of never seeing my people again, but Father Stone's road won't yield. I make a decision.

"Follow me." Passion bleeds into Father Stone's voice, infusing it with energy. "Know the true way, the one way, eternal salvation." He reaches out his hand, a gateway into his world, a chance to walk only one road, to end my lifelong division: one road, no blending, no Native traditions, no *Anishinabe*.

I stay still, refusing his hand. If I walk into his world, I will never see the *Anishinabe* Otherworld. If I go with him, I will never see the hint of happiness. If I have to stand here for eternity with my feet in both worlds, at least I can still see my people. The roads in my mind uncross, straighten out, converge and diverge, one red, one white. I pray to the Great Spirit for the strength of my people, the *Anishinabe*.

Father Stone looks down, just for a moment, then looks back at me quickly. He's tired.

"Take this cross from my forehead. I'll outwait you. We've done it many times before."

His face sags, but his eyes burn. He's a beacon, an Other-worldly source of power, fueled by a conviction greater than himself. His mouth is pressed in a firm, determined line. "I can wait forever," he says. "I have eternity on my side."

"Great Spirit," I whisper, "Please resolve this. I can do no more. I give it to you." I am shaking. If this man discovers an opening of weakness in me, just a second's worth, he may drag me off to his white world forever. I think of our Great Spirit, of Father Stone's God, of his Christ, of my own Ojibwe, joke-cracking Christ. I've prayed to them all in my lifetime. They blur together like the red and white roads. "Please help me."

The cross on my head is throbbing, sending jolts of pain into my ghost of a skull.

"Take my hand," whispers Auntie Lacey. She stands before me: large, powerful, sharp. The tiny crucifix gleams as she pulls the rosary over her head.

My left foot tingles, coming alive. I look down. The red road is clear, focused. The *Anishinabe* are close.

"We believe what we want," she says, "but we will never let the traditions die."

Auntie Lacey walked the tangled roads more gracefully than I could have imagined. I remember her cabin, with a picture of Christ hanging next to a dream catcher she'd made. *Why did it never cause her the torment it caused me?*

"Rebirth yourself," she says. "Walk the road you choose."

I reach out and hold her fingers; they are weathered and warm. She presses the rosary crucifix to my forehead and pulls it away, drawing out the ash cross. Auntie Lacey lets go of the rosary but it doesn't fall. It hangs suspended over the two roads. The crucifix turns, sending glints of light in all directions.

The left road firms up beneath my left foot. The right fades and blurs, and Father Stone is a shifting silhouette, though his eyes still burn and his mouth works wildly. Wild rice rushes up before me, a panorama, surrounding me as the white road on the right drops away and dissolves.

A great pressure falls away. Clarity shines into my mind. I walk onto the red road, my hand in Auntie Lacey's. The relatives crowd around, greeting me, joking, speaking the language of the People.

"*Mii gwetch*, Great Spirit," I whisper, my nostrils filling with the nutty smell of parched wild rice, my feet in one world, finally belonging.

everywhere

e buried Ma on a morning when the dust was swirling so high it brushed my shoulders. Daddy and my Aunt T. Tonya took turns digging, and I tried to help even though I'm only a seven-year-old girl. Ain't as if I'm not used to hard work on this homestead. But we was all not doin' so well with the digging, and Daddy was getting weaker from the lack of food. The dust kept filling the hole in. We gave up; we could barely breathe, and the last part of my Ma I saw was her bare calf as we turned her into the shallow hole. Dark hair matted against her blue cheek. Her nightgown, gray with dust, fluttered around her ankles.

"Coyotes'll get her," I whispered.

T. Tonya pinched me hard on the arm. Her hands was bony like claws. When she first showed up here, she was plumper. She's from the city, my ma's sister.

Daddy turned away from the grave; he wouldn't look at me.

"Ain't no coyotes anymore," hissed T. Tonya in my ear. Her breath smelled like old cigars.

Weren't as strong as we used to be, Daddy and I.

. . .

Ma never talked about T. Tonya before she came here. T. Tonya showed up on our doorstep right when Ma was beginning to fail. I thought my aunt was crazy. She'd been heading to California, but she stayed. T. Tonya nursed my ma and sang her strange sad songs. Ma said T. Tonya talked to the spirits. "Promise you'll take care of her," Ma whispered from that raspy throat of hers. "She ain't like to be part a this world." Ma could barely breathe, yet she wasted her strength talking about the crazy woman. "Take care of her. Feed her. She got nowhere to go."

Daddy's face got hard, and his mouth went into a thin line, makin' his lips all pasty white.

No one had anywhere to go. We saw them all, straggling across the prairies of dust, walking or driving junk heaps, but mostly walking—heading west with the hope of jobs in California. No one stayed put except us.

"This is my land," Daddy said. "It's all I got. I ain't leavin' till I die."

"You ain't ever leavin'." T. Tonya's eyes scrunched up, hollow and cold at the same time. Her hair was glass rivers of red and gold. "You'll haunt this place till the end of the world."

I growed up working next to Daddy, stacking wood he chopped, planting our yearly garden, skinning and butchering game. I knew it from my bones that the land lived in my Daddy, same way it lived in me.

. . .

Dust blew through my dreams, billowing across the plains in clouds of black and gray, reaching to the sky. Grit stuck in my teeth; I choked on the dust. Lightning cracked, unseen. Darkness covered the world, and coyotes screamed and yapped at the heavy sky.

A bony hand, a small hand, touched my shoulder, lingering.

"Ma?" I whispered.

"She's here," hissed T. Tonya.

I jumped, thrust from the dream. T. Tonya lay on top of my blanket, on my bed, next to me. Her eyes glared hungrily in the dark, reflected from the low slant of a moon through my window. Chills raced up and down my arms, and the hair on my forearms stood up with goose bumps. I fingered dust out of my eyes. It came in everywhere, through every crack in the house.

"Your ma doesn't want to leave," whispered T. Tonya.

"You'll wake Daddy." The dust had formed a mask on my face, hard, like the same look Daddy got when he talked about the land. My face would break if I thought about Ma.

"She's here. I done talked to her spirit," said T. Tonya.

Won't let my mind go that way, won't ask about Ma, won't think about Ma—

I jumped up, and the bedsprings screeched, sharp as my Daddy's saw on a deer leg bone, clattering like the ancient cars full of hopes, running from the dust. I ran away from T. Tonya's reminders of Ma; I ran outside, where I knew she wouldn't follow. She didn't have the land and the dust in her blood. The coyotes howled. T. Tonya was wrong about anything real—they were still here.

. . .

I followed their songs, harsh, yipping, blending, and winding in a high spiral. Their hard yips were as real as the dust, as the earth beneath my bare feet, as the cool smoothness of something I tripped on.

A bone: long, curved, a leg. I held it and stroked it and sighed, relief exploding from my chest. The bone was old, weathered, dry, bleached smooth in the droughty sun, picked clean by ravens and crows. *Real.*

"We ain't gonna make it," I said to the sky, and those words was real, too, as hard as the cries of the coyotes.

Daddy and I walked farther every day, looking for food. Nothing grew in the ground. It was gray and dark like the sky, covered with dust and parched as bones. The game was less and less, dying or moving on. The only animals that survived was the ones Daddy called "the scavenger ones": coyotes, ravens, and vultures. We'd eaten blackbirds and squirrels when we could get 'em. Was a time I can barely remember, and I hang onto the memory of when things was green here and the garden grew and we had cattle and deer for eating and eggs. Don't remember the taste of an egg now.

"You got to hang on," T. Tonya whispered behind me.

I whirled. She trembled in the dark. The coyotes sang again, and her shoulders jumped. Her eyes stayed big.

"My daddy hangs onto the land," I said.

She put her hand on my shoulder again and hunched down, trying to look hard into my eyes.

I pulled away, turning toward the sound of the coyotes. The outline of an abandoned farmhouse, our nearest neighbor, was so black I couldn't make out the windows. It'd been so long since I seen a star. "Daddy says they didn't have the land in them like he does, like I do." I looked at the farmhouse.

"Hang on for your ma's spirit," whispered T. Tonya.

But the dust rose up in me and made walls around me. "She ain't here!" I cried. "She's dead and gone! We buried her in a grave, and you were there, and we turned her into the ground, and the dust covered her. Ain't no such thing as spirits." I knew if I started believing Ma was around in some spirit way, some ghost that draped through my dreams; I might never have the strength to go on and face what was real—the coyotes and the dust and finding food and wood and surviving, if we could.

"I don't want to believe!" I screamed at her, and I left her standing there on the barren ground, a tiny woman who sang dark songs, the coyotes yipping in anticipation.

. . .

My daddy and I hunted the next day. We kicked up dust, walking past the abandoned Cramer farmhouse. Long since, we'd cleaned out what our neighbors left behind. We'd butchered the cattle they'd left to starve on the field, but without enough salt to cure all that meat, much of it rotted. Carcass bones pushed through the dust, buried and curving toward an unbroken horizon of gray.

"T. Tonya, she followed me outside last night," I said.

Daddy's eyes held me like frozen water. "Why?"

"Daddy, why don't she ever go outside? What's she so afraid of?"

He flexed his fingers. He had his rifle slung over his shoulder. We was gettin' low on ammunition. I'd overheard him tellin' T. Tonya. They didn't think I heard, and they didn't think I saw them when they took from their plates to give to me. We all went to bed hungry, but they was hopin' I went to bed a little less hungry than them. I never said anything; we all gotta have somethin' to hold onto.

He looked out way across the dusty field to where gray dust earth met gray sky. You couldn't tell where the dirt ended and the sky began. The dust brought it all together.

"T. Tonya wasn't born to the land," he said finally. "She don't understand it."

Dust swirled around our feet. The wind was pickin' up as it got warmer. A raven screamed near or far in the gray. Dust made distance all equal.

"She said Mama's spirit is hangin' on," I whispered, and a huge rock slid off my chest. I took a deep breath and coughed.

"That's the only thing real to her," said Daddy. His cheeks looked hollow, like dusty valleys on his face. His eyes was always tired.

"We ain't gonna make it, are we?" My hand started to tremble; I shoved it in a pocket dirty with bits of scrap and wood and lint and dust. Grit pushed under my fingernails.

He turned to me. He looked down and met my eyes. Them clothes hung on him like he was a corpse. All that moved him was bone and skin and wiry will. But the beams from his eyes, they seemed to spin like the dust clouds when they come pounding in from the distance. "Don't know, hon," he said softly, "but we're doing our best and not givin' up." The skin around his eyes, it softened for one second, and the tiny lines around his eyelids, they seemed to blur and disappear.

"I ain't givin' up on you," he said.

Them coyotes started yippin' again right then. They screamed at each other and answered, and their voices spun crazy toward the dusty sky.

"Mama's gone," I whispered, and my words made me strong, hard as the parched dirt under me. My words pounded beams into the ground. "Ain't listening to T. Tonya. Her spirit talk makes me crazy." And that's all I could say. I couldn't tell him her talk made me all unraveled with sadness so big it hurt to keep it inside. I couldn't tell him how I wanted to hang on, too, but needed to find my own way. I didn't know the words.

He took my hand, bone against bone. "She's everywhere," he whispered. "Your ma is everywhere."

Dust tickled my ears. I blinked, and it fell from my eyelids, scratching my face.

"Ain't nothing more real than that," he said.

I breathed out heavy. Weight slid from my shoulders.

Ain't no spirit walking in the way of my Ma. Ain't no ranting of a crazy city woman who we feed and keep safe, even though she don't know the land, don't know the feeling of standing on it and being it, having it come through your calves and bones and rise up into your heart: dust, sky, gray, dirt—and some days rain and green again. I knew it as my Daddy said it. My Ma is here in the land, real as the dust we breathe, as the clouds that roll in, as the field of bones, real in her death, even though she goes on and on, sky and land that never end.

heart armor

"You here again, Sandra?" Marty asks without surprise. His tattered lawn chair creaks as he rocks, and strings of green and white plastic hang from under the seat. Marty looks like a gentle old guy in baggy pants, but I can feel his bottom-line pragmatism. I feel *way* more than I should, especially when my reserves are getting low.

Marty's got a box terrier in his fenced front yard, and his house is a row house, old housing built for the miners when iron ore was king in this town. The sky is gray with high, thin clouds; the air is cold and dry in the middle of the day. If the wind is blowing the right way, you can smell a mixture of wood and chemicals from the pulp mill. More people move away from here all the time; there's not enough to hold them. Business is slow for Marty, but customers like me help.

"You got a high-maintenance heart," he says. "Ain't many like you."

"Yeah, I know." At least he won't give me the tired old crap about how I've got to be tougher, as if I can change how I am.

"People like you are my best customers." He grins, and a chill snakes up my back.

Too bad. My parents told me I was one in a million. Others need heart armor too, but not to the extent I do. Even harmless remarks hurt when they were directed at me. Some don't need the armor at all. *Lucky bastards.*

"That'll be $400," Marty says. Behind him I hear the hiss of the town steam heat system.

I'm damned lucky to still have a job around here. I could go to the city, but I'd have to buy really heavy armor I could never afford. My friend Pete had a heart almost as soft as mine. He committed suicide last year when his reserves got too low.

"I can't afford this," I plead.

Marty's eyes glint. *"You don't have a choice, do you, sucker?"* He did let me have armor replenishment for nothing last year when I got in a pinch and the mine laid me off for the season. Marty understands the boom-and-bust cycle of mining.

I sigh, pulling out crumpled $100 bills from my jeans pocket. I'm careful not to look at him; I don't want him to see how hard this is to pay for. He might use it against me in the future.

Marty puts his hand on my chest, muttering the spell that will provide a casing to protect me; heart armor. Now everything will hurt a little less. I won't feel that burning in my heart that lingers like acid. I won't have to cross my arms in front of my chest; a useless reflex that I've never been able to break. The armor comes with a cost; it dulls my circulation and my senses. Everything looks fuzzy. Food tastes blander, lights are dimmer, and life is muted.

"Good for a month," he grins and stuffs the bills into his pocket. He pauses for a moment, and I think I see shame flash across his face; but it's instantly hidden, and the armor is already doing its job; I don't feel bad for him. "By the way, kiddo, I'm leaving. Not enough business in these parts. I'd have to charge people like you a fortune."

He walks into his house and shuts the door.

. . .

I move. I have no choice.

The month between that last armor replacement and the move is hell. The armor wears off twenty days and eight hours later. I can't even get my money back. Marty is gone as the wind.

By the end of the month, my senses are screaming. I want to crawl into a warm bed and never come out. It hurts to go outside and look at the bright sunlight. My heart burns with the slightest provocation, even the offhand, grumpy remark. True anger, directed at me or others, turns my chest into a furnace. I want to move to the middle of nowhere.

I tried that once. Moved way to the country, with no people around for miles. Yeah, it was cheaper, and I only needed armor once every six months, or maybe seven months. Fewer people equaled less hurt.

But my heart felt cold, and that scared me. My senses went dormant; it was worse than the muting from the armor. I couldn't feel, taste. I didn't care what I saw, and I couldn't remember it.

I ended up in this mining town that's not desolate and not city, but something gray and in between. When I drive out of town for the last time to move to the city, I see the bars on the main drag with shabby signs in need of a paint job. The landscape of the mining town gets smaller in my rearview mirror; squat and plain with identical row houses, surrounded by hills of taconite tailings.

. . .

It's been too damn long since I've been to the city. I've forgotten my defenses. My chest is burning with the emotional bombardment and noise and stimulation. I need to find an armor salesperson soon.

First, I rent a hotel room with a cheap weekly rate. It's an old building on the edge of the city with Murphy beds that pull out of the wall and make the living room into a bedroom. A small bathroom and closet are adjacent to the living room.

Next, after walking through the skyway system and passing people who look as if they are professionals, I find the temp agency. The temp agency people give me a ten-key test and an application. They tell me I'm fast on ten-key, and low-wage operators are always in demand.

There's a nice job for me too with very little one-on-one people contact. I had a teller job once. I couldn't deal with the emotional bombardment of the customers, of the coworkers. Don't have to watch out for people and lose energy keeping my guard up. It's likely that if I get the ten-key job, I'll be working in a cubicle by myself.

The temp agency sounds hopeful. One of their clients needs help keying thousands of student loan applications, and they should be hiring a bunch of temps in the next few days. I hurry out of the office. My reserves are low. I don't remember ever feeling this shaky.

A silver Lexus careens around the corner, running a red light as I'm crossing the street. "Bitch!" the driver yells, and my hands shake.

A cop car roars out of nowhere, sirens screaming, turning right in front of me and flying down the alley I was about to cross. It's a K-9 unit, and I see a large German Shepherd in the back seat. The car slams to a stop, and the cop jumps out, grabbing the dog and yelling at some guy who's pressing his body up to a building in terror. I can almost smell the dog's fiery breath. The dog snarls, and I imagine those jaws ripping into skin. Stars fly across my vision—little shooting lights—and I lean against a wall with a wave of faintness.

There's an armor salesman on the corner a block ahead; I can see the telltale red hat. These city armor salesmen have a recognizable code, a uniform. Maybe there are more here like me who need the armor—fast.

I'm hobbling by the time I reach the salesman. He puts his hands on my chest. "High maintenance, right?"

I nod. The salesman does his magic, and I'm fortified for another month.

.   .   .

It doesn't go the way I planned. The city's hard on me.

The temp job for the student loan processing center comes through. I walk to work the first afternoon, second shift. On the corner, newspaper vending machines sit in a row of six, alternating blue and green metal casings. Their paint is scraped. Headlines from six different papers spell out variations on the same news— another suicide bomber blew himself up. Inwardly, I feel the pain of a twenty-one-year-old life and the lives of all his victims cut short by a bomb ripping flesh to pieces. And then there is my own helplessness, but what can I do?

My new boss introduces herself and assigns me a cubicle. These cubicles are used by real workers during the day, and I'm an imposter. I push aside a memo and notice a photo of children. I can't help it; my chest starts burning again, and I feel that shaky tingle in my hands. *What would it be like to have children, to smell their newborn baby skin, to love them, and to feel their anger and rebellion and passion?*

I've got to get to work. I put the photo face down and start keying, and the ten-key's all wrong.

The numbers are reversed. It's the kind of ten-key that's set up like a touch-tone phone, not a calculator. There's no way I'm going to be able to keep my usual speed. I'm panicking. I need this job. *They're going to find me out!* My fingers stumble as I pick up the first green and white triplicate student loan application. It's hard to see the numbers in the dim fluorescent light in this windowless place, this borrowed workspace. The world is closing in.

Am I really sitting in a room full of darkened cubicles? I hear ten-key operators tapping around me, sounding fast. I push myself, entering the numbers, watching them flash up in predefined fields on the screen. I'm sweating because I know that after this night, I won't even have this temp job. Plenty of people right behind me need jobs, too, and are probably a damned lot faster than I am on this machine. The supervisors monitor our output and our errors. My armor is thin, very thin. It feels as if I'm twenty days into the month already, and I've only had the new armor for a few hours. I hadn't counted on all the stress. I feel for the people who need jobs; I'm angry at myself for fucking up; I'm scared I may not be able to afford to live in the city.

A scratching sound on the top of the cubicle divider makes me look up. A guy is there, giving me a curious look, running his wrist along the rough material that covers the dividers. His watchband catches on the fabric. He's got dark, wavy hair, and he's looking straight at me. Something in his eyes looks familiar. It's like the look I've seen on my face when—

"Break time," he says. "We always take a break at six thirty."

. . .

The windowless vending machine room has the same dingy glow as the rest of the building. It's hard to believe there is an outdoor environment with real light and darkness. Next to a machine with candy bars and crackers is a small microwave. The door is hanging open, and inside it I see dried cheese, crumbs, and salsa smudges on the greasy glass tray. The guy sits with me at one table; a gaggle of women are at the other table. I don't see the supervisors.

"I'm Kyle," he says.

"Sandra." I'm stirring a cup of the vending machine coffee and wondering if I'm going to regret drinking the stuff. Kyle is pulling open the plastic wrapper from a sweet roll. I'm surprised to see a guy in this crowd—a cute guy. He doesn't look like a second-shift ten-key operator. He should be a stockbroker, maybe a model.

"So, this your first night?"

I have no idea whether he's really asking or just making small talk, so I nod yes. There's muzac in the background, murmuring forgettable sounds.

He's playing safe, asking innocent, distant questions, and I'm glad. It's been so damned long since I talked to a guy who's got a flirty look in his eyes. *You're a dolt. How do you know he's attracted to you?*

We continue talking. How long has he been here? How long will the job last? I don't tell him I think I've fucked up my chances to keep this job. Maybe the supervisors just don't know it yet. There's something about his eyes; they're drawing me in. I look away.

There's a pang in my chest, and it hangs on a moment more than usual. His eyes remind me of David, whom I dated several years ago. David had the sensitive act down well, very well. He said the right things to make me believe him. I almost gave my heart to him, but never again.

Kyle starts to ask me another question, but I'm saved by the women. They get up as a group, and I realize our break is over. Everybody heads back to the cubicles where the ten-key machines are waiting. I feel Kyle's gaze on my back, and my armor shivers. I'd like to believe he's nice. It's been a long time.

.   .   .

At the end of the week, they let me go.

"Why didn't you mark on your application that you'd only done the other kind of ten-key?" the supervisor admonishes me. I can't tell her that when I filled out that original application at the temp office, my reserves were dangerously low, my armor paper thin. When that happens, I don't think straight, and I tend not to notice the small details such as different kinds of ten-key.

I don't see Kyle when the shift is up that night. Maybe it's for the better that there are no necessary goodbyes.

● ● ●

The temp office doesn't call the next day or the next. The city noises outside my hotel room are harsh and loud; my nose burns with the pollution in the air. I have some money in savings, but I need it to last for several months if I plan to stay here. Everything is more expensive in the city. I head to the job service office and post a resume. Trash on the sidewalk crinkles beneath my feet. The dusty windows of an abandoned factory building reflect dull sunlight.

There's a cappuccino shop on the next block, and I duck in, thinking that maybe caffeine can give me the jolt I need.

Kyle is sitting at a booth; he looks up and sees me before I can back out. "How you doing?" he asks. His laugh lines make crinkles around his mouth.

"Fine." My heart is hammering. I hope he doesn't hear the shaking in my voice. If he finds out, he could hurt me. It's been a long time since I let myself get close to a man.

And I'm low, I remind myself. There's a draining feeling of urgency when this happens, as if I can feel the heat in my chest pulling down further into my stomach, radiating throughout my torso.

He orders cappuccinos and insists on paying. I'm too tired to object. I sip the hot, rich, milky liquid and feel gradual strength seeping back.

"Did anyone ever tell you that you look like Meg Tilly with blonde hair?"

Sweet talk, I tell myself. *Don't listen.*

So I smile and play dumb and change the subject. He couldn't possibly be interested in me. He goes along with it, and then I'm feeling the protection kick in again, the feeling of armor starting to thicken, even though it has to be my imagination.

The music on the stereo system has changed abruptly from jazz to classical: "Pachelbel's Canon in D."

I've got to get out of here. I never listen to music that makes me cry when my armor is low.

Kyle notices. "You like classical music?"

Before I can stop myself, I'm nodding. I jump up and make some excuse about feeling sick.

"Give me your phone number," he says. His eyes hold mine.

I scrawl it on a napkin with the pen he offers, ripping the thin paper, and run out before he can get a good look at my face.

· · ·

The temp office calls the next day. The rep on the other end of the phone sounds crotchety. "Got a client who needs the type of ten-key *you* do," she says. She gives me the details as I sit on the hotel bed, drawing spiral patterns in the cheap bedspread with my finger. I'll start next week. It's a long-term assignment, and she acts as if she's doing me a big favor.

I try not to let myself get mad. It'll just wear out the protection sooner.

"Just don't forget, there are plenty of people out there who need jobs," she reminds me.

There's $500 left in my savings, and it's not going to last forever. I feel the sour burn traveling from my chest into my torso.

The phone rings the minute I put it down.

"Want to go out?" Kyle says.

My heart is hammering. "Sure." What's there to lose?

"I'll pick you up at seven. Dress up." He won't tell me where we're going, even though I ask three times.

· · ·

Shit. Oh shit.

A doorman who's dressed in a cape and top hat holds open a glass door with a polished gold handle and frame. Kyle heads for the ticket booth. He looks great in dress pants and a sweater. I see women in gowns, people in jeans, carpeted stairs that remind me of a southern plantation house, and rich woodwork. People are holding drinks in plastic cups, munching on biscotti with cappuccino.

Why the hell didn't I get another armor replacement before we went out?

Because, fool, I tell myself, *you had no idea he'd take you to the opera.*

Kyle smiles and hands me my ticket. I'm ready to bolt, but the sheer emotion of the place has frozen my feet to the fine, carpeted floors. Somehow, I manage to follow Kyle to the theatre auditorium. *La Traviata.* Mezzanine level.

"Box seats," says the usher, as she hands us a richly illustrated program.

"You look beautiful tonight," Kyle says.

Tears spring to my eyes, and I look away, hoping he won't notice. I've got my hair up in a French braid. It suits my face. My fingertips sizzle, and I wonder how far the armor has worn down. *Why didn't I try to look frumpier? You're defenseless,* I tell myself, *completely defenseless. Stupid girl.*

Kyle smiles at me again. His eyes are green, like mine. "*La Traviata* is one of my favorites," he says.

Mine too. My heart is pulling me here, chaining me to my seat, even though my feet and my mind are telling me to get out now. We are, as the usher promised, in the mezzanine box, and we have it to ourselves. The other two seats are empty.

The orchestra tunes, the conductor comes out, and the first measures of the overture fill the hall.

. . .

I lose it in the third act. Violetta is singing. It's the first time I've cried in so many years. They're bursting to get out, the tears. My hands tingle with the emotion of the singer. Her crescendos, her climbing scales, are pushing me over a mountain of joy and fear and passion. And I feel my heart—completely raw, exposed.

Kyle reaches over and puts a hand on my shoulder then pulls it back quickly. He hands me a Kleenex from his pocket. "What's wrong?" he asks.

"My armor's down," I blurt before I realize what I've said. I can see the moisture in his eyes; we're near enough to the stage to catch its light.

"So is mine," he murmurs. "Has been for years." He takes the crumpled tissue from my hand.

I stare at him wide-eyed. Violetta and Alfredo are reaching the climax point of their duet in Act III.

"I don't use it anymore," he says. "I'd rather feel."

Before I can stop myself, my hand snakes toward his. His fingers are long, sure, firm. The singers' voices rise and follow, entwined in duet, spiraling, cascading, setting each other free.

transcendence

rudy bustled around the basement kitchen of the Baptist church. A devout member, she regularly attended the Wednesday night Bible study, legs crossed in polyester pants, breasts and torso straining her white blouse. Trudy took her Bible study seriously and sat in the sessions every week, her gray hair styled, one plump finger pointed on the page being discussed, her hand tracing the verse.

This Wednesday night, a perceptible air of tension and excitement simmered in the building, traveling to the church basement where she now arranged bars, cookies, and other confections on faux crystal plates. Trudy dabbed a crumb with a wet finger, licked it off, and wiped her finger on her pants. Behind her the giant percolator worked itself into action, the force of its heat making it bubble like an awakening volcano.

"Hello, Betty," she called out. Were the rest of the Lutherans here?

Betty put down a covered platter; Trudy could see the lemon bars that pushed against the tight plastic wrap. The sound of feet pounded and shuffled through the ceiling. *The church must be getting crowded.*

Betty pushed her glasses up on her nose, and Trudy caught the lone reflection of a Christmas tree in the lenses. Upstairs were more trees and lights—tastefully done, so as not to detract from the *real* meaning of Christmas, the birth of the Savior. A Nativity Scene decorated the altar area.

Betty exhaled. "I'm glad this only comes once a year."

Can't the woman be happy? Trudy decided not to ask why.

"What are you singing tonight?" asked Trudy. Creamer and sugar were set out; everything was ready for after the program.

"A reworking of 'Ave Maria.' Very challenging. The sopranos have to sing a high G."

"Really!" Trudy made her face look astonished. The Baptist choir could hit a high G with gusto. "Aren't you glad you sing alto?" *Too late. Will Betty take it as an insult?*

Betty appeared not to notice. "Thank goodness. I can barely hit C above middle C."

Trudy nodded. She didn't sing, but she knew enough about music to know what would happen tonight. It would be a lovely program. All six churches in town would present music that celebrated the birth of the Savior. Some of the smaller churches would sing, but they were always spotty, with poor accompaniment or none. The Baptist choir would excel as it had for years. Even the Lutheran choir wasn't bad, for that matter.

Betty pulled her coat around her. "I've got to get upstairs."

Trudy could hear the sounds of various choirs warming up, singing scales that ascended by a half step with each repetition. The noise was like the cacophony of a school band.

"Good luck." Trudy arranged everything a last time on the counter so people could pass through in a line, taking bars, cookies, coffee, napkins. Then she headed upstairs.

. . .

Largely unnoticed, the Catholic choir clustered in the back of the church finishing their warm-ups. The groups consisted of one bass, two tenors, four altos, and three sopranos. Unbalanced at best, but what could you do in a small church? Their director, a youngish woman with dark hair and a face that was distinctly un-Scandinavian in this northern Minnesota locale, surveyed her group, trying to think of any final tips to give them. Nona was not religious but loved vocal music so much that she'd been talked into directing the choir when she moved here. The choir looked nervous, but Nona also saw a lust in their eyes—a lust to succeed.

This was her second year with this choir and her second year in this small town. She was well aware of her role as an outsider, and these heavy religious events made her uncomfortable. However, she was sure of her ability to connect with this choir. She'd taught them everything she knew about technique and the emotion of singing. The rest was up to them.

Nona said to Ben, one of the basses, "Remember, breathe." Ben had a bad habit of running out of breath and taking in more air in the middle of a word. And the bass singer was highly unpredictable; his voice was either glorious or flat enough to throw everything off. Nona wasn't worried about the pianist. Moira did a good job and actually listened to the choir. She'd saved them a couple times and covered vocal gaffs with her quick thinking.

"Keep your mouths open on the vowels. 'Only in Joy.'" Nona mouthed the words from the choir's piece, drawing out the vowels in each word and mimicking the appearance of a relaxed jaw line with the breath behind it to—hopefully—support beautiful sounds. "Enunciation. Good consonants, but not overdone."

The church quieted. Time to sit down. One last morsel of inspiration.

"Use your faith." Nona whispered to her group. "Sing from your faith." She felt like a hypocrite talking about a faith she didn't share, but she knew it might be the key for this choir.

. . .

Trudy sat near the front next to her friend Gail Brevanen. The two women chattered under their breath, Gail's birdlike face contrasting with the ruddy fleshiness of Trudy's cheeks.

"Don't they look great?" The women watched the Baptist choir line up to move to the front of the church and sing the opening piece.

"You were right to allocate the money for those new robes."

"They look like angels."

"And sing like angels."

"Unlike *some* choirs."

"I heard Rudy Swanson takes a drink before he sings."

"Maybe that's why he's always flat."

"Hard to find a good male voice."

"Did you hear Arla is thinking about leaving her husband?"

"No! Why?"

A voice overrode the women. "Welcome to the annual Christmas choral celebration. We gather here in the name of Christ."

Silence draped itself over the church, and the various mutterings faded out. The Baptist choir strode up to the chancel. Trudy prepared to enjoy the music.

The pianist hit a chord, then launched into a bluesy gospel intro. Three measures later, the choir jumped in, swaying with the beat of the music and the passion of their belief. Some audience members clapped in time; more daring souls moved their shoulders and upper torsos. By the time the song soared to an ending crescendo, which featured a high B flat for the sopranos, the crowd erupted into applause.

"Wonderful, wonderful!"

"The best."

"Our choir puts the others to shame, doesn't it?" Gail whispered in Trudy's ear.

"Ssshhhh," said Trudy, thinking the same thoughts. She sighed as the next group ascended the chancel, A choir from one of the smaller churches.

"Why do they insist on putting us through this every year?" she muttered. Their belief was strong and deep, but enough was enough.

Gail shook her head. The group, consisting of several adults, two children, and a baby held by one of the women, didn't have a pianist. They stumbled through an *a cappella* version of "What Child is This" with the baby wailing midway through the song to the end. Relief flooded over Trudy when the group left the chancel.

"Who's next?" Trudy laid out the program in her lap.

"Our Lady of Peace." Gail made a face like a pained kitten.

Trudy hoped the damage would be fast. This choir was almost as bad as the fringe churches.

. . .

Nona's leg shook as she led her choir in front of the chancel. She stopped and faced the group. They formed a small semicircle toward the audience.

Why did I ever take this job? Was the love of music worth humiliation? She could hear the whispering in the audience and was glad she couldn't see the people behind her. Nona knew enough about past performances to imagine what the whisperers were saying.

"This choir isn't so hot."

"Always off key."

"They just can't get it together."

She took a deep breath, wishing she were anywhere but here. Nona's shoulders knotted with tension. She hoped the audience couldn't see her knees knocking through her black pants.

She raised her hand to begin conducting.

The whispering stopped.

The Our Lady of Peace choir took a breath, relaxed their jaws, and released a beautiful, on-key "ohh" vowel sound that was perfectly in sync with the piano. Inside, Nona felt a small part of herself tighten with the hope of magic, afraid that if she let it go, the moment would shatter and disappear.

Only in Joy
I have peace that is mine
This is the gift
Of the Savior

The choir crescendoed to "peace" and backed off slightly to descend to "mine." They sang with open, full vowels, giving a rich sound for a small group. Nona thought she felt something akin to shock settling onto the audience behind her.

"Ohhh," she whispered to herself, "let it be."

They sailed smoothly through the second verse, and Nona could barely keep from grinning. Then they exploded into the chorus.

Fireworks erupted inside Nona. The choir roared through the church, shocking the audience. They nailed the "t" on the end of "not" with a surge of passion. They didn't need her!

Emotion spilled from the group. It electrified her and the stunned townspeople like a current of pulsing purple and orange and blue energy that Nona could actually see. With relief and a giddy happiness, she watched the light pour from her choir, falling like blinking stars onto the townspeople's heads. Nona laughed aloud, turned around, and looked. No one seemed to notice, least of all her choir who grew and grew in sound until they sounded like an eighty-person, fully balanced group. Ben was on key and strong enough to balance the big sound from the women. The sopranos had lost their thin tone on the high notes; they sounded like trained, full-bodied opera singers. Nona wanted to dance on the sparkling light that fell from the ceiling. The audience was silent, transfixed by the music. Maybe she could like living here. Nona raised her hands and thanked a higher power for the passion that her choir had grabbed, molded, and expelled into this light.

They ended the song, slowing to a sweet, sonorous *pianissimo* that was barely audible. It was saved by the choir's enunciation of the last word, "away." The group sang as one, with enough vocalization on the "ay" of the last syllable. Nona held her breath, waiting for the beautiful sound to die away, wanting it to stay, knowing it could not last, wanting never to leave the moment of light that had transformed the church. Slowly, the light ebbed away from the singers and floated to the ceiling, easing until it had vanished and no trace remained. She felt the pressure of growing sadness within her.

Silence in the church. Nona could see and sense the wonder drop off, the shock set in. Astonishment registered on the faces of the people as they considered the next move: to clap or not to clap?

They began to applaud, a stunned synchronization of palms smacking skin. To Nona, it did not matter whether they'd applauded to raise the roof or refused to clap completely. She and her choir stepped from the chancel into a new world. She fearlessly put her foot into the new dimension, a composite scene where the light remained dancing around the choir, the audience, and Nona with its unearthly purple, orange, and blue highlights.

.   .   .

In the church basement, Trudy busied herself behind the table filling coffee cups for the crowd. Lucy poured punch.

"Good program." Mr. Byronson took a cup of coffee and loaded his plate with a brownie, a lemon bar, a piece of cheesecake, and several Christmas cookies. "You Baptists brought down the house as usual."

Trudy allowed herself a small smile. It had been a good program, though entirely predictable. The groups that always excelled gave wonderful performances. The not-so-good groups muddled through, like that church out in the woods and the Catholic group—

She shook her head, started to say something to Gail, but then thought better of it. Trudy couldn't remember the Catholic choir's piece. Unusual that none of them seemed to be down here. The Catholics never missed a party.

Out of the corner of her eye, Trudy saw a dancing light bounce from the ceiling, brilliant with electric purples and blues. It tugged at her memory, but she was unable to make the connection before it disappeared, replaced with the sameness of the scene around her.

the day jaded came to town

A woman's voice sliced through my dreams, low and cold. Ice raced to my core. "Call me Jaded," she said.

Her words cut like a chainsaw. Jaded loomed over me, big, shapeless, powerful, with eyes the color of slate and black hair straight as boards. Her hands were callused and big enough to kill a man. The smell of flint rose from her shoulders, and as she brushed against me, I trembled.

Then she smiled. Her lips made a river of blood. My insides collapsed. I sweated bile.

I woke with the sheets stained. My easel stood in the corner, untouched for thirty years since I took art lessons with Lila Peterbow.

Lila Peterbow went missing the day I woke from that dream.

Jaded came so fast; we never had a chance.

. . .

Six of us sat in the café, guys I'd gone to school with, or the dads of my friends. We were bone tired after the second day of pushing through tangled swamp and forest, looking for signs of Lila Peterbow. Sweat dripped from my hair down the back of my neck. The smell of wet popple came from my hands.

"Bobby." Lila's voice echoed down hallways, smudged by memory. *"Such talent."*

Ceiling fans did little to make the place cooler, and the old hardwood floor creaked as the waitress moved between tables, taking orders and pouring coffee. Our imaginations ran black as we'd searched for Lila: body parts; an arm, stretched to the sun; a mutilated torso; what the forest would yield.

Jaded's mocking breath brushed my back. *"What have you been, Bobby? What could you be?"*

The men's eyes had the dull look of Jaded. Jaded had tingled against me as we pushed through the snarl of swamp plant and tamarack bog. Around our café table, I could see her in the downturned lips of men, in the dull clank of a coffee cup against a saucer, the hopelessness like a heavy fog.

"Try again tomorrow," muttered Albert, next to me. Albert had been my dad's closest friend. "Whadaya think, Bobby?" Albert was a month from retirement; same as Lila's husband Herbie.

"What do you think, Bobby?" Jaded mocked.

"Yeah," I said.

The box factory had given us yesterday and today to search. No pay; we did it for the community. We did it for Herbie Peterbow, whose life had been turned inside out.

"Dogs lost the trail on the road," said Robbie. "Maybe she got turned around in the woods."

We hoped.

The smell of flint brushed my cheek, and I shivered. I looked at the streetside café window, and for a moment, I saw the ghost of her big face in the reflection of the café window. Then it disappeared in the slice of the sun.

"See something?" whispered Albert.

I shook my head, staring at the plate.

We all knew what a lost trail meant.

Mikey coughed, deep from his throat. "Katie's afraid to go out now. Makes me sick. Around here."

Jaded's blood lips smiled in my memory, and I heard her laugh again.

.   .   .

"Don't let me die like this! Oh God, not this!"

Lila's emotions spun trapped in her mind, a discordant three-part invention playing over and over. The body had gone beyond shock. Physical pain transmuted as her thoughts and fears whirled in a screaming melee.

"Don't let me die alone."

Helplessness seized her, weakened her, gave her despair beyond the greatest anguish. "Don't let me die alone." She grieved for Herbie. There would be no closure, no folding of the laundry, no cup of coffee to send him off to work.

Her body was easier for her to look at, easier than grieving a husband she might never see again. The attacker had grabbed her on the Peterbow's own road. She'd been out picking berries and thought nothing of it when the clean, new sedan pulled up and a man asked for directions.

Jaded's laugh ground against what was left of Lila's spine.

"Go away," Lila whispered weakly.

Picking the berries, that bright red burst of raspberry, eating one for every ten; falling off the bushes into her pail; falling onto the ground. Lila had worn long pants to shield against the thorny tangles of the raspberry bushes. Now her legs were bare, her body raped and left to die. She could not move; bones were broken or muscles paralyzed. Her mind raced, running out of time, hoping the world would remember her.

Stupid to trust a strange person, but who'd ever grabbed anyone out here? Lila would pay with her life for her naiveté. The fear would build, a force that people sensed in each other.

Oily, flinty breath came hard against Lila's skin.

Lila wished she'd carried a gun. She wished she'd kissed her husband when she last saw him, before she left to pick berries. She wished she could paint one more picture of ladyslipper or bunchberry or the bobcat she'd seen creeping at the back of her field. She wished she could see the sun instead of the moldy rotting walls of this outbuilding where she'd never be found. Pain coursed around her spine like a double helix. Lila passed out as her attacker opened the creaking door of the outbuilding and came back in.

. . .

We went back to work after a week of searching and no leads. Herbie Peterbow sank into depression and wandered the house, unable to sleep. Relatives and neighbors brought him food and helped him with the day-to-day stuff.

The cops called off the official search. We walked the woods, searching for Lila, but gradually our numbers dwindled. Life's obligations—jobs, kids, commitments—turned Lila's memory into a fading shadow.

On a cold morning, I walked toward the café. I blinked, and Jaded towered above me, laughing with heartlessness, real as the pavement I walked on, real as the yellow brown sun. I smelled her. I touched the black leather of her jacket.

In a blink, Jaded dissolved. Flint lingered in the air.

. . .

"Katie's started carrying the nine mill when she walks," said Mikey.

I grew up with guns; been hunting deer and grouse since I was ten.

"We're turning into the city," I said. "Soon everyone will be locking their doors."

Albert shook his head so hard his glasses shifted on his nose. "Nobody wants to come here. No jobs. Too many mosquitoes."

The winters were long and cold; change would never come. Change was happening though. Jaded visited me in my dreams that night. She towered over my bed, close enough to strangle me. The easel in the corner looked like the skeleton of a forgotten town.

"Lila Peterbow will never be found," Jaded hissed. Dry wind swirled, and moonlight spilled over her, a cold cape. Night sky through the window turned to burning blue, then to the slate gray of an early winter. Grass grew at her feet and shriveled, curling into stringy brown tendrils. Her voice ground like sawgrass. "Fear will take over," she whispered.

I shook my head no. I'd grown up here; it was my town.

"You think you know so much, don't you?" she said.

My voice froze in my throat.

"Your town will turn into one more place where people don't care." She laughed, and I tried to hang onto something beautiful; one of Lila's landscape paintings, Lila's flowers on canvas.

"Go away," I slurred. "Leave me alone."

Jaded left slate gray in her wake, but her deadness pressed in, an unwanted lover. The easel sat, unmoving.

. . .

The small part of Lila's consciousness that lived was glad she could feel no pain. Death closed around her, a vacuum. The attacker, big and dull-looking, approached her with his knives. Lila moved in and out of awareness. *The body is gone, destroyed,* she thought, *but there is still me. There is still what I was—painter, wife, woman.*

He came closer now, and his eyes were blank, no less horrifying than the first time she'd seen past the smiling façade, the first time she'd realized he was something other than human.

"Don't forget me!" She cried out to her husband and the town and her friends and everyplace she'd ever been in her life. "Don't forget who I was, what I did. Don't forget!"

Time expanded, and the vacuum closed in.

. . .

The waitress brought our coffeepot, and we passed it around the table, pouring, sloshing it over the rims of the cups. Albert dumped cream and sugar into his.

"Katie's been dreaming," said Mikey.

I shivered.

"You've been dreaming, too, Bobby."

Jaded's breath caressed my innards with greasy, sticky deadness. I squinted at the café window. Jaded towered over parked cars, arms folded, feet in black combat boots.

"Katie's been dreaming about Lila."

Jaded's breath grew hotter, grinding against my gut. The men fidgeted. The glare of the sun slid behind clouds blowing in.

Mikey ran his words together. His voice rose, his hands moved. "Lila was in a cabin. An old rundown cabin. Blood everywhere."

My head tingled. Wind rattled the glass in the café windows and shook the floor. Jaded laughed with that smile that ran rivers of blood.

The waitress stopped, tray of food balanced on her forearm, and blinked, her jaw slack.

"Lila was mutilated, all cut up."

I exhaled heavily and stared at my food. The café floor tilted.

"Lila said we shouldn't forget her. We shouldn't give in."

"Shouldn't give in to what?" said Albert.

"Don't give into fear," I whispered. "Don't give into Jaded."

The café windows rattled like brittle leaves, and I thought I saw the ghost of giant tumbleweeds hissing up and down the street. These days, the blue sky had a steely sheen; the old-timers said it would be a hard winter. Walls went up. We stopped saying hello. We stopped asking about wives, kids, lives. We went within. I could drive down any road in town and the front doors were shut, refusing my entrance. We were out in the cold with only the gritty company of Jaded for consolation.

Jaded lingered in the woods at night when dark rolled in, and I didn't go out to look at the sky full of stars anymore. I watched them through the window without the bite of the air to make them more brilliant. The Northern Lights looked weak and sickly green. I locked my door at night now and slept with my rifle next to the bed. When Fred Olson died after a battle with cancer, no one stayed long at the wake, and no one cried. Unfinished casseroles, cake pans full of lemon bars, and plates of chocolate chip cookies kept the ghosts company in the church and mortuary.

. . .

"Bobby. Bobby!" The voice cut through my dreams.

I thrashed, half asleep, half awake. "Go away."

I waited for the sick feeling that would slime my innards, for the smell of flint, the bloody smile.

"Bobby, I want to be remembered."

"Lila?" I whispered, my eyes wide. I focused, adjusting to the darkness. "You're okay!"

"I'm dead, Bobby." She stood by my easel, hand on its side. Moonlight from the window behind her spilled through her and poured onto my bed.

"You're whole," I murmured.

"Nothing matters now," she said. "Did you know I can paint forever? Oh, Bobby, if you could only see the possible beauty! I can mix the most magical colors. And gardens! All I've painted are flowers. Lily of the valley, iris, butterfly weed, phlox, verbena."

My heart ached. "Lila," I said, "there hasn't been much time for beauty since you disappeared."

Jaded's laugh simmered, flinty and hard.

"I can't move on," said Lila. "Herbie's holding me."

Jaded laughed again, and steel ran through her voice.

"She's holding me too," Lila said.

"She's holding us all." I knew it as truth the moment I spoke it. The wind picked up outside, and the window shook. The moon turned colder than blue. The grip of sharp, icy fingers came tight around my neck.

"Help me, Bobby," said Lila. "Help me paint."

"Lila. I can't paint. I haven't painted for so long."

Jaded's laugher hissed like electricity, and her hands stayed around my throat.

"Together," whispered Lila.

Warmth ran through my arms and hands, contrasting and tingling strangely against Jaded's cold and gritty presence.

"Together we can paint this," Lila pleaded.

"No one will remember you," crooned Jaded, and gritty dirt laced her words. "Another amateur artist. A housewife picking berries in the woods. They'll remember you for bringing the first big crime to town and nothing more." Jaded's cruel laugh echoed through my house, through the woods, all the way into town, and Lila cringed.

"They'll remember me if they don't lose hope," whispered Lila.

"No." Jaded's deadness rode on the wind. The closed front doors of houses rattled in their frames, and dust pounded passersby who narrowed their eyes and headed for home.

"Help me, Bobby," Lila whispered.

Through Lila, I saw Herbie. He had lost weight and stayed inside the house, sitting by the phone. Herbie cried and groaned in his sleep, dreaming of the variations of Lila's death. He forgot to eat.

"Help me save him."

Jaded clamped tighter around my neck, and I choked and gasped for air, but Lila guided my hands. As we painted, I had no idea what spilled onto the canvas, but the colors became brighter, and the lines flowed and blended, and gradually, Jaded's grip around my neck loosed and disappeared.

"You can move through grief," Lila whispered to Herbie. He stirred in his sleep. "Beauty remains."

· · ·

I knocked on Herbie's door and gave him the canvas. "From Lila and from me," I said.

He looked at me as if he understood. I looked at the canvas for the first time. Images burst from the surface in a blend of Lila's style and mine, all of it beautiful: the turn of a stem of ladyslipper; the tenuousness of the dew that clung to the underside of a blade of grass; the puffy black and white of the chickadees, hurriedly feeding on seeds before winter set in; the call of the geese heading south, high in the air in a near-perfect V; a bobcat, prowling the edge between field and woods.

Herbie cried until his throat was raw and his voice gone, but the grief was deeper now, and healing.

· · ·

"Go," I told Jaded, and Lila moved within me. "There's no hold for you in a place where people feel. Go."

Jaded retreated, her cold eyes cuttingly discerning.

"I'll be back," Jaded hissed.

"Go," I said. "People care. It hurts them but makes them more human."

Jaded left, and only the brittle rattling of leaves on the street hinted at her departure.

.   .   .

In the fall, I scouted the woods for the upcoming deer season, looking for a good place to put my portable stand. A rotted outbuilding, its lopsided door hanging ajar, froze the breath in my throat.

The door pulled me in; my knees shook, and a burning sensation raced through my arms.

"Ah," I breathed, a core of numbness growing within me.

The corpse was dismembered, chewed by animals, caked in dried blood. I saw the look of discovery on her face, eye sockets open and staring skyward.

.   .   .

Our paint strokes healed the town. The sky smoldered with a warm red/blue hue, even with the bite of the coming winter. Front doors received the warmth of the day, and lights glowed yellow from the windows at night, shades open. Katie stopped carrying a gun when she walked and admired the reflection of the sun on the last of the aspen leaves. We waited for the tamaracks to turn gold, the last of the fall color.

We meet for breakfast in the café and ask about each other. We say hello on the street. We don't forget these things: the beauty in a moment, the anger at a bloody violation, the caring that makes us human.

detours

My wife Emilia calls me the walking lie detector. When any-one beats around the bush, I see squiggly lines—real lines, in front of my face, invisible to everyone else. The lines look like a road map gone berserk. So much of my life, except for my inventions, has been indirect routes or squiggly detours. My inventions are my truth; no bullshit. Working on them gave me some of the only times I've seen straight and clear lines.

I've always invented things. I'm ninety-four, and my love for dreaming up new things will never change. Emilia looks at a doorbell and sees a doorbell; I look at a doorbell, and I'm putting plans together in my head. That doorbell ends up part of the home security system I'm designing for our apartment.

"Why don't you just buy an alarm system? We've got the money." Emilia is thin and birdlike. She could be my bride of twenty, she looks so good.

I'm a Yankee. Why buy when I can take old parts, combine them, and create something new? She knows that. She's egging me on.

"Gotta protect the place from the leaf peepers," I answer. The foliage is excellent this year.

"Leaf peepers don't come here."

Emilia's right, of course. Leaf peepers go where the leaves are: Vermont or maybe New Hampshire. I'm putting up the alarm for...

I don't remember.

My mind's empty, and I look around, and I'm not sure where I am. Someone is staring at me with a concerned expression. The straight lines have turned in on themselves; twisted jumbles that go nowhere.

Emilia. Emilia. I repeat it until it begins to sound familiar. I take a long breath. Sweat beads on my forehead.

"Jacques," she says. "What's wrong? What are you seeing?"

I shake my head. How can I describe the winded roads, the new routes my mind is taking? I don't know where they'll take me.

. . .

We're getting ready to go. I can't remember where. Emilia lets me off the hook.

"Remind me to take that crossword puzzle book back to Deb's tonight."

Deb and Regis, our best friends. We must be going for Sunday dinner.

"Deb loves those crossword puzzles." Emilia is chattering, pacing the apartment, her small feet pushing into the sculpted rose carpet. She burns calories like I burn twisted roads through my brain. "Me? I can never figure those puzzles out. The little boxes drive me crazy." Now she's covering a cake with foil. It's frosted with chocolate, but someone's had a piece of it, and the yellow cake part looks moist. "Get ready, Jacques," she says, "Deb likes to serve dinner at five."

Boxes and lines and dinner on time. It seems there's another reason we're going to dinner, but I can't quite remember it. I keep seeing the schematic for a lawnmower engine or maybe a special hinge for a rumble seat.

Emilia remembers. "Regis wants to tell us something."

.   .   .

I don't know when I started seeing the lines—actually seeing them and not just knowing they were in my mind. Maybe it was twenty years ago, maybe a year ago, maybe I was a chubby, dark-haired, four-year-old tot.

"Where are you?" Emilia snaps. "Off in dreamland?"

I shrug and give her a confident smile. The steering wheel seems high.

Emilia's doing the pedal dance on the passenger side. Her feet shift back and forth on the blue floor mats. She stomps her left foot on an imaginary brake pedal. The cake pan slides across the back seat and hits the door with a soft thud. "You almost sideswiped that car!" she yells, voice cracking. There's a white van pulling in front of us.

"Maybe he shouldn't have been passing."

"Don't you ever use your side view mirrors?" Then Emilia gasps. She stares at the window, then stares at me, something like horror and admiration flashing across her face. "When did you take the mirrors off?" she whispers.

I don't remember. I'd like to know how long it took her to notice. Why keep something on a car you don't use, anyway?

"Ch-ch-ch," she says, in a scolding squirrel-voice.

.   .   .

Deb takes the cake from us, but her face is tight, and the lines around her are jumbled messes. Regis and Deb's home is thick with detours tonight. Something churns in my stomach. I wish I were back in my old shop. *Do I still have a garage?* In my shop, the lines were short and direct.

"Jacques." Deb runs a slim hand over my shoulders. "You're looking good. Have a seat. This chair will be easiest on your back."

I feel something simmering below her words. *Where is Regis?* The room is dancing with the tangled lines, and I'm beginning to lose my balance, even though I am sitting down. Deb is already setting food on the table: lasagna sliced into serving pieces, salad, French bread.

"Where's the dynamite?" Emilia jokes, referring to a local type of sloppy Joe, but spicy and served on hot dog buns.

Deb shrugs, sits down. "We had dynamite last night."

Regis comes out of the bathroom, and something inside me closes and becomes cold. He looks yellow. The lines around him remind me of my mind: unfocused, jumbled, a big mess.

"Jacques." He smiles, but it feels forced.

Deb serves him two slices of lasagna, but she looks twice at the plate.

"You get your roof fixed, Jacques?" Regis asks.

The silverware the four of us are using is clacking quietly on the plates—*click, chonk, tink.* The table is cherrywood and polished; Deb is an immaculate housekeeper. Not a thing out of place, not even the lace tablecloth.

I reach back through the jumbled lines in my own mind to try to remember. Deb is giving me a strange look. There's a thread I see somewhere in the mess, and then I have it. Jacques' son Jason was supposed to fix the roof. I didn't let him.

"I patched it myself," I say, and the lines are tight, defiant, like taut guitar strings. "Why should I pay someone to do it?"

"Jacques!" Deb is horrified. Emilia shrugs her shoulders; she's used to me getting my way.

"Jason needed the money." Regis looks a little less yellow for a minute. "He could have done a better job. Why don't you have him do it the right way? You're too old to be messing around on the roof."

Now I'm mad. "I can still mess around on the roof if I want."

Regis sags. He's yellow again.

"There's something," says Deb. She's talking too softly. Usually she's chit-chattering. She's thin too. Burns all her calories worrying and pacing like my wife. I'm caught in a tangled ball of yarn that no one else can see.

"Regis is not well," says Deb. She's having a hard time getting the words out. Her eyes look older than the rest of her face.

An abrupt *clonk* pierces the silence as a spoon bounces on a plate.

Regis is staring at his food, and his arms are hard against the sides of his chest, forearms crossed. "I have cancer," he blurts.

The lines in the ball of yarn are straight and parallel.

Cancer. The word cuts to the bone, to the center of the lines, to the center of us all.

"It's not so bad," says Deb, and her voice is too bright.

Emilia sits back, staring at her food like it's the enemy. The world is the enemy.

Cancer. I turn the word around in my head. *How does cancer feel?*

Deb's mouth is working to keep from crying.

"Lung cancer," says Regis softly.

I'm staring at my food and thinking of its passage through my body. *Where are the lungs? What does this mean?* I can't remember the words. I reach out to take Emilia's hand, and it's thin, papery. Her hand is shaking, and I grasp it firmly, not sure why.

Deb draws her breath like a sharp knife. "We'll fight it," she hisses, and the red rises up around her like a warrior shield.

Fight what? My own lines are blurring and jumbling again, like the lines around all of us.

"You should have let Jason fix your roof," says Regis.

. . .

"That was a lovely dinner, don't you think?" Emilia is

chattering as we drive home, but her voice sounds tight and distracted at the same time.

It's raining, and I can barely see the crowded flats. "People don't bother to paint their houses anymore," I mutter. There's an old three-story on the corner of Third Avenue and Fifth Street. I remember a time when that house was well kept, had a weeded garden, a time when it looked as if the people who lived there made an effort.

The aftertaste of lasagna in my mouth reminds me of dinner. I remember long silences and tangled lines that skirted the truth; I remember Deb's lacy tablecloth.

"Regis is sick," I whisper.

Emilia's staring at me. She'd like to say something, but the silence I've created doesn't let her in. She's frozen to the passenger seat, her thin, veiny hands straight as boards, pressed into the upholstery.

"I should be the one who's sick." I'm ninety-four, twenty years older than Regis. I'm supposed to die first. The car's climbing up Fifth and the hill is insanely steep, more like San Francisco than the east coast.

"It will be okay," Emilia murmurs. Her hands clench and unclench, and she flexes her fingers. The silver wedding ring is impossibly loose, and the diamonds slide out of view, transiting an endless circle. The only straight line I can see is the path of the car.

. . .

Regis goes in for tests. Regis goes in for pre-op. These words mean nothing to me as Emilia repeats them in a hollow voice that holds no promises. Regis will go for surgery. He will start chemo.

I've never been in a hospital in my life except when I was born.

"Don't trust those doctors!" I holler at Regis over the phone. The lines are straight and black around me for one clear moment. "They'll pump you full of poison. Fight it on your own. Cut to the quick."

Regis is silent, though, and the empty noise on the phone makes me think of a kid who won't step on the cracks in the sidewalk. Regis is putting up walls to turn the pain into nothing. I have a brief vision of a fairytale book from a long time ago; a book with pictures of a circular tower that could not be scaled. Its bricks were thin and polished, making it impossible to climb out or in.

"Jacques," Regis says, his voice heavy. End of conversation. The jumbled lines are still there, but they stop at the wall.

· · ·

We're driving to Regis and Deb's house again. It's probably Sunday. I can't remember, though there is a plate of cookies in the back seat, covered with foil. They're Emilia's iced cookies, and she's decorated them with Halloween colors.

Can Regis eat, I wonder? There's been talk of eating and not eating; I can't quite place the details and the times. *Why are we taking food?*

"He'll stop eating tomorrow night." Emilia's words are short and clipped.

Regis's surgery must be coming up soon. Then they'll start the chemo. I remember being told this was the order, but I don't understand why the order matters. It's all confused from day to day. The only thing I understand is the straight line I'm steering the car in.

"Jacques!" Emilia shouts.

My foot comes down hard on the brake.

I jerk my head up. I narrowly miss hitting a car coming from the opposite way, making a left turn in front of me. I'm not sure whether the light was green or red or if it matters.

"You should let me drive."

I'm imagining cookies all over the back seat, orange and black decorations settling into the crevices. Emilia would have it cleaned up in a minute if we were home.

"Sorry," I whisper. I've got to hang onto what's straight, not jumbled and confused. Not like the lines that have been around all of us lately. My face is set. My hands grip the wheel. I want to cut through the haze and the tangled mess. I don't remember everything. I don't understand everything, but I can always see the lines.

We're on Regis's street. *How did it come up so fast?* He's the only one who keeps his house up. The rest of the flats look shabby, in need of paint jobs or mowing or trimming. I can barely make out Regis's house among the jumbled lines.

"Oh, Emilia," I murmur, and the sadness in my voice chokes me up. "All the detours."

"What?" Her voice is sharp, an accusation of my craziness.

"I can't see his house."

I feel her eyes on me, angry and worried at the same time, but I'm looking straight ahead. Through the massive net of jumbled hopes and fears and intentions, I can hardly find the house—the nicest house on the block. Deb's a real fusspot, always puttering in the garden, painting the fence, keeping things clean.

"Here," I whisper.

Emilia's arms are rigid. Regis's driveway is narrow with a fence on the left side and a high stone wall on the other. It barely accommodates my car, even without the side view mirrors.

"Jacques. Slow down!"

This straight line is all I have. There's a slight twist I need to take at the end in order to get the car in the right place, but with the straightness, all is clear.

"Emilia. I can see!" They're dancing in my head now, the inventions and the designs. There must have been hundreds of them. *How long has it been since I've seen them all?* A blueprint for a solar collector. A device for taking hot things out of the oven. The rumble seat I invented even though none of my great-grandkids believe me. I wonder if they even know what a rumble seat is.

I gun the engine. We're flying in a straight line, lifting in the air, and everything is clear.

. . .

"Jacques! Emilia!"

Deb's banging on the car door. Rain is running off the window, off her hair, pouring from the roof and hood of the car in great waterfall gushes. For a crazy moment, we're fish in an aquarium. Emilia's fine, just startled. Deb's pulling at the door and manages to get it open. We crawl out past the steering wheel and stand in the downpour, taking in the scene. Regis comes up with an umbrella and for the moment, he has some color. The car's in the garden, two feet lower than the driveway. Deb tells me I drove through the fence, and I look behind me. Two feet up, over the stone wall drop-off, the picket fence is on its side. I give Deb an apologetic look.

"It's okay, Jacques, but what were you thinking?"

"He sped up." Emilia is shaking her head. "He really shouldn't be driving."

I'm thinking about the shortest distance between two points, a straight line. I'm thinking of the clear feeling of flying toward the truth.

. . .

Regis goes through his tests and his surgery. He's weak and pale, and the lines around his house are thick and curvy, detours that lead to a jumbled mess. They rarely straighten for me these days, except for certain moments of clarity: when Regis is sick and has to hurry to the bathroom; when news comes from the doctor that is definitive and that we all understand at the same moment. The four of us look at each other, no detours in place, only the straight lines to our fear and our love, the straight lines to our hearts.

dad's rural genes
a memoir

My dad is no longer alive to talk about his rural dreams. When Dad was alive, I didn't know enough about country living to be interested. I suppose this is one of those bittersweet Scarlett O'Hara moments when I realized what I had, or might have had, only far too late.

When my father died in 1997, my brothers and I had to clean out his house and go through each and every paper and article he possessed. We found Dad's journal, and we read his writings. I don't know if this was ethical, but I do believe Dad would have let us know if he was displeased. I say this because he did let us know, after he passed over, that he was okay. But that is another story.

In these journal entries, Dad wished he'd spent some time living on a farm. I don't know if Dad meant actually doing the hard work of farming or homesteading or whether he simply had the romantic vision of rural living that so many people have. Knowing the ups and downs or the hard work and the rewards of country living is impossible until one has actually experienced it, but I do think it is interesting that Dad had that rural dream inside him.

There's an old picture my brothers and I discovered when we were sorting through Dad's stuff. It's a photo of Dad's parents walking out into their backyard garden in Meriden. Dad's parents were not rich, and the house was humble, but the flower garden was incredible. Flowers of all colors, some as tall as my grandparents, surrounded them as they walked out into their small yard.

My grandparents' love of gardening was passed on to Dad (and eventually to me). Dad filled his tiny back yard in St. Paul with vegetable gardens and some flowers. When Dad's muscular dystrophy made it hard for him to get up and down, he had raised beds built so he could sit and work on his vegetable gardens.

I cared little about gardening (or country living) at that time. My husband and I were still in the city. We did create a tiny garden and started some seeds in the house though.

Dad may well have made a wonderful homesteader if he'd had a healthier body or if he had someone to share household work with. He harvested many of the vegetables from his garden and canned them. At the time, I didn't have the slightest interest or understanding of food preservation. Three years ago, I canned my first salsa and was extraordinarily proud of myself. My husband Chris had canned for several years prior to that and still does, but Chris grew up in a family that regularly grew and processed food on their rural New Hampshire land.

Dad was always shoving home-processed jars of chutney under my nose, trying to get me to take a taste. The chunky brown texture of the chutney repulsed me, and I refused to try it, though I may have been being stubborn just for the sake of being stubborn. I'm a lot like my dad that way; I attribute it to his full-blooded Polish heritage. Polish heritage may well have shaped Dad's rural genes, especially since our ancestors were peasants.

Frugality, also part of Dad's rural genes, was a quality I used to disdain. Gradually, I discovered that frugality could give me freedom. If I didn't have to buy a new car every three years, then Chris and I didn't have to earn that money. There didn't have to be car payments, and I would have more time to write. Dad understood pinching a penny, and while there were times he may have gone overboard, it's another one of those Scarlett O'Hara things. I wish I had understood and respected his frugality better when he was still alive.

I hope Dad is watching the homestead in the country that my husband and I have created with hard work and love. I hope Dad is smiling when I track our expenses and decide to forgo one thing so we can have another. I hope Dad is pleased with what we've saved for the long-term. I hope he approves of our land steward-ship choices: when we put minnows and ducks in our pond—rather than chemicals—to clean the pond up; when we burn dead grass so it doesn't get dryer and become a huge fire hazard; when we scavenge firewood so it doesn't go to waste; when we barter; when we provide our neighbors and ourselves with fresh eggs from our laying flock; when we take the time to camp and be in the woods; when we gather berries and harvest venison; when we labor for sheer pleasure with no agenda. Thank you, Dad, for your rural genes. Are you listening? Are you watching?

farmwoman

ever thought they'd take the land from me, Ritchie. Thought I would always hold it in my heart. You told me the land would never leave me. Told me to my old, wide face with sunken eyes and a babushka around my head, as I watched you, my husband, get smaller and smaller. Life left your body, your hairless head shrinking deep into a hospital pillow. Life drained from you fast, a torrent of autumn turning quickly into the death of winter and cold. I wanted my body to shut down; to follow yours like two foxes weaving through our field, fluid and clever, merged at the torsos, red plumy tails waving in the air. But the life force kept coursing through me like the stream that bordered the back of our ten-acre homestead. The homestead's gone now to someone who bought it and tore it down and put up a fancy new house. I'm living in town in a two-story apartment building for old people. Each apartment has a porch that faces frozen Bailey Lake. It's my aim to sit on that porch and freeze to death, to join you.

My arms are folded hard against my chest. You always said I looked like I "mean business," that I'm "one tough cookie." The ice on the lake is blue with cold. I've an old black coat on, and that same babushka I wore when you were dying in the hospital. When I was younger, I had thick brown hair. When it grayed, it grew thin and wiry with disorder. It reminded me of the way my life spun apart ten years ago—when you died, Ritchie, and when I was forced to leave our land and come to this dull, terrible place.

Always thought these porches were useless. No one sits on them. People might put a potted plant out or two, a geranium or a sprawling fern. Two porches down I see stringy brown fronds of a frostbitten and dead fern, left to die in the cold.

Wind stings my cheeks. I have sturdy shoes on, shoes made for working, not for pacing in an apartment for old people. Same shoes made endless circuits of our homestead kitchen. Shoes are like new; I had 'em resoled because we couldn't afford new ones. Canning. Freezing. Nursing sick hens, hauling water to animals.

My blood will freeze.

We are all made of rivers, rivers of blood flowing through veins and arteries. We carry running rivers inside us; our breath is the wind that makes the aspen leaves dance. We breathe, and I hear the wind, a storm coming in from the west, low on the flat horizon. Rivers and breath have always been part of me, just as they were part of you.

Snow blows in tiny tornadoes on the surface of the blue lake ice. I've been alone in blizzards with none of the buffering concrete and buildings of the downtown. None of it ever scared me. I lived for storms; I hummed with the electricity that came from the air. We hunkered down in our cabin, designed small before "ecological" was a word and before "being green" was a fad. Put it up ourselves. When the hard winter storms came, we sat close to the woodstove, watching the mutating orange flames, reading or talking, working on a puzzle, playing dominoes.

Winter was time for cutting and splitting and stacking wood, not for pacing in a town apartment, trapped with artifacts collecting dust—photographs and things people think old ladies like. Becoming an artifact.

Canning jars, seed starts, stretching a dollar. I did it all well, as any good farmwoman would. And when they came to take me from my place—my niece and her kids—I was outside on a day much like today, stacking wood, the wind biting fiercely at my face.

I can still feel your big gloves slipping around on my hands, Ritchie, as I grabbed the wood. There's an art to it or the pile will fall over, much like working a puzzle. Every piece of wood—maple, aspen, birch—is differently shaped. Aspen splits clean and even, as does maple. Birch is tougher and full of splinters. Maple and birch are less "stemmy," easier to stack. But knotty and jagged wood can be stacked to create a thing of beauty, and any country person driving by will admire the depth and symmetry of the woodpile.

I didn't see Anna's car at first nor hear it approach on the thin layer of crunchy snow and ice. I should have known; that niece of ours visited once a month, and it was time again. I was intent on my work. When I stacked wood, I got like you did, Ritchie, focused and in my own world. I got lost in it, like we both did, deep in the woods, picking blueberries in July.

The car door slammed. I dropped a split piece of aspen. It fell on my work boot, but dry aspen is light. It glanced off my foot into snow.

"Aunt Haney!"

I focused. Anna stood next to the hood of her old Buick, a dirty reddish brown color. Her two teenagers stayed in the back seat. They huddled together over something, ignoring me and their mother.

"You shouldn't be stacking wood!" Anna grabbed a piece of aspen out of my other hand. "You could fall! What are you doing out in this weather?"

"Hand me another piece," I told her. I wanted to get the stacking done before the snow really started coming down. I had things to do inside.

Anne glared at me. "Did you split this yourself?" Her thin face got longer, jaw ajar, eyes alarmed and questioning at the same time.

"Wouldn't hurt you to split some wood neither," I muttered. "What are the kids doing back there?" Their hunched backs were still visible from the window.

"Text messaging," Anna said.

"What's that?"

"You send messages on your cell phone."

Messages on cell phones? How many messages does a person need in one day? You loved my stubbornness, Ritchie—said it kept you strong. I tried to feed you my fire in the hospital, but ain't nobody stopping death. Nobody.

"You shouldn't be out in this weather. We'll get you an apartment in town," Anna said. Her voice caught.

I glared at her. She knew what she was doing was wrong. The kids crouched over their cell phones, typing with thumbs.

"Don't take me from here," I whispered. "This is all I have and all I want." Cold wind biting and telling me where my body begins and ends, wood to hold in my hands, canning jars bright with tomatoes and carrots and beans against the sun on pantry shelves.

"Aunt Haney, you can hardly walk!"

I walked fine, just slower than others. Didn't hurt to slow down. I could still carry wood with.

"I worry about you here all alone."

And I looked at her, her face that looked so like my own. We will all be alone if we wait long enough.

"This is MINE," I said, eyes burning. "All I have left."

She wasn't listening. She had forty-two-year-old ears, ears that still had much to learn. She was pulling on my arm, leading me back to the house, the kids in the car bent over their cell phones, the car running, its exhaust swirling into the air, mixing with the snow. I gripped a piece of aspen tight.

. . .

I gave into her, Ritchie.

You married me for my temper, but that temper's become diluted with time and with all the stuff of life pressing in. There's more to keep track of now, Ritchie, and I don't know how anyone can handle it alone.

We were young and strong, hardworking, when we bought our land. The world was quiet and simple. We wanted to live in the woods. We'd both grown up in the country, watching our fathers build chicken coops from salvaged wire and wood and metal sheeting, learning to grow and can food before we were ten. We could find a storm in the sky, hear the land groan with drought or billow with water fat, shoot the wing off a fly at fifty yards with open sights.

Footsteps crunch below my town porch. Two walkers out in this cold, walking on the lake path, passing under me. I hold my breath, as if they might hear me. Sit still, not hard now that my body is feeling cold and dull all over. Except for my fingertips, which feel warm. There is no feeling in my face. This won't be hard, Ritchie. I've become invisible in the city.

We walked, too, Ritchie. Sometimes we tramped in the woods behind our house on an old logging trail. More often than not, we were working together outside. When you died, Ritchie, I missed how you talked to the hens and they cocked their heads and listened. You were the sensitive one. You hated to butcher. You said words over the animal and wished it a peaceful passing. You were the person closer to God than anyone I've ever known, even though we weren't believers and didn't waste our time at that gossip-fest of a church in town. "Why go to a church?" you said. "We're close to the spirit of the land. It's under our feet, in the trees, in the tremolo of the wind, in the cleansing rain, the bite of the snow."

The spirit of the land is here, Ritchie. It catches the river running out of me, chunks of frozen blood in a river, mixed with my life force.

There's an end point, Ritchie, where a stream feeds into a larger river or where it stops, forming a pond. No one knows where the headwaters begin. Fresh water seeps slowly from the water-fat land in years when we have enough rain. These are the places, Ritchie, where I feel myself heading now. I'll form a headwater of blood and bones, of new beginning and gray hairs, of memories that mean nothing to anyone but me and you, of efficiency and harvest, of a steady aim with a pistol. Meet me there, Ritchie, in the headwaters place, where the world is neither young nor old, where the only messages are merging love, merging love.

about the author

Catherine Dybiec Holm is an award-winning writer and a yoga instructor. She lives in rural Cook, Minnesota, with her husband Chris, on 10 acres in the boreal forest. Although the Minnesota northwoods have been her home for the last 15 years, she spent the first 35 years of her life in large cities. Moving to the country awakened her desire to write. She began freelance writing and editing in 1995, and started writing short fiction and novel-length fiction in 1998. The impact of moving from the city to a remote rural area continues to shape her writing; and magic and surrealism often show up in her stories. She enjoys living close to the land and experiencing wild landscapes everywhere.

Her short stories have been published in several anthologies and chapbooks, including *Dust & Fire*, *Fantastic Companions*, *Electric Velocipede*, and *Spirits Unwrapped*. Currently she is working on a novel and a memoir. To learn more about the author, please visit www.catherineholm.com.